I0456851

# Contents

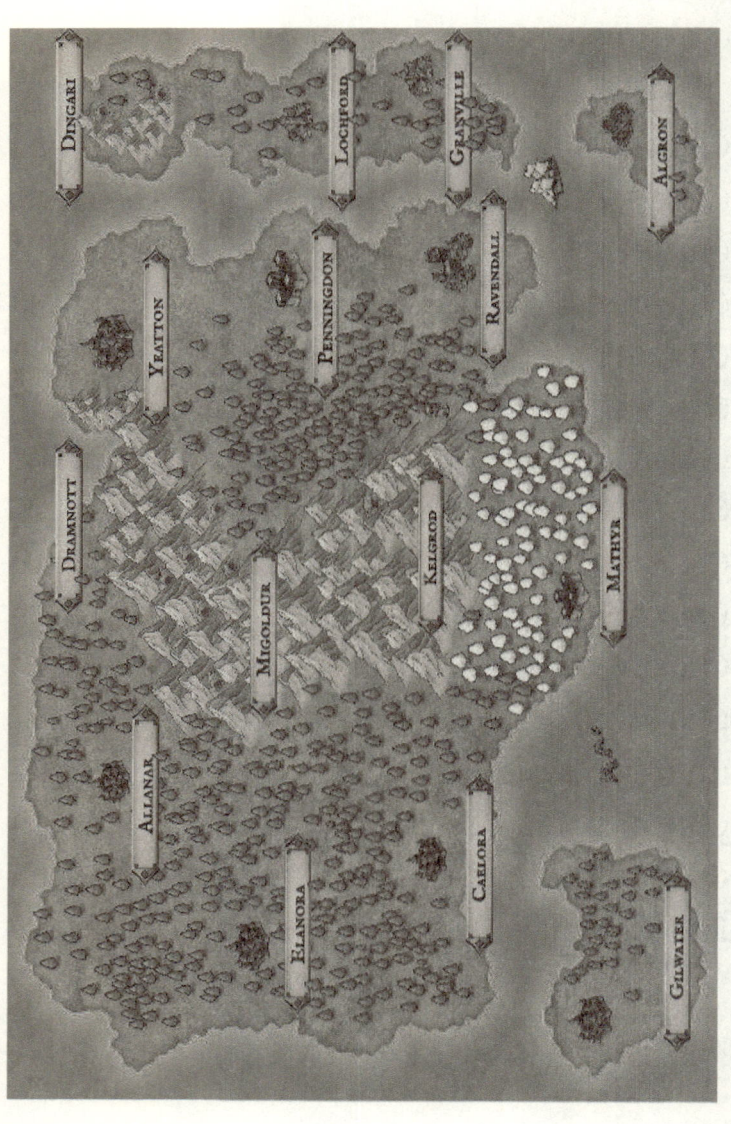

# Tricking Beauty

## RIVER WOODS

Renaissance
Valley Publishing

© 2023 Renaissance Valley Publishing

All rights reserved. No part of this publication may be reproduced, distributed, or transmitted in any form or by any means, electronic, mechanical, photocopying, recording, or otherwise, or stored in a database or retrieval system, without the prior written permission of the publisher.

Published by Renaissance Valley Publishing

ISBN: 978-1-7367947-7-7

Florence, Alabama

Visit our website at www.renaissancevalleypublishing.com

The characters and events portrayed in this book are fictitious. Any similarity to real persons, living or dead, is coincidental and not intended by the author.

If you purchased this book without a cover, you should be aware that this book is stolen property. It was reported as "unsold and destroyed" to the publisher, and neither the author nor the publisher has received any payment for this "stripped book."

Woods, River

# Tricking

# Beauty

# Chapter 1

P rincess Nixa felt a single tear slide down her cheek. She touched the surprising droplet and wiped it away. "Where did that come from?" she thought. She wasn't a crier. Logic ruled her actions, not emotion. No one else would have considered it unusual, though. After all, she was burying her father.

The court gathering around her at the gravesite probably thought it stranger that she didn't shed more tears. Though Nixa knew she must have some feelings for her father, deep down, she had never really felt them on the surface, especially since he had remarried. Mostly, they had avoided each other. Apparently, she cared more than she realized.

The funeral ended, and Nixa slipped away into the trees. *After all, what was more natural than a grieving daughter wanting to be alone with her sorrow?* Nixa thought with a snort. Her stepmother could deal with the court and the other mourners. She had her son to support her; she didn't need the princess there.

Nixa wasn't leaving the crowd to grieve, though. She was leaving to plan her next move. With all her sad smiles and crocodile tears, her stepmother would be thinking of the same thing. Who was going to rule the kingdom now?

Nixa slipped quietly through the dense forest of tall, towering trees. The scent of freshly fallen rain, damp earth, and mossy logs lingered in the air, calming her mind and clearing the turmoil of her rapidly rushing thoughts. She stayed to the shadows that danced around her like a soft embrace, enveloping her in a blanket of darkness as she moved confidently through the trees.

She made her way to the clearing, ducking behind an old oak as soon as she arrived. Moonlight blanketed the area with its silvery hue, making it appear to shimmer in its soft glow.

In the center, an old hunting lodge stood, its wooden exterior weathered from years of disuse. A thick layer of ivy snaked around its walls and roof, and the shutters on its windows hung loose. Nixa paused and glanced around cautiously before hurrying across the space and into the dark building.

A man waited inside, filling the room with the pungent odor of an unwashed body. His long, scraggly hair hung over his shoulders, matted with dirt and oil. Nixa resisted the urge to wrinkle her nose in distaste. She must not offend until she got what she wanted.

"Well?" she asked abruptly.

"No one will touch her," the man replied sheepishly.

"No one?! No one at all? Not even for the amount of gold I'm offering?"

The man shook his head. "The queen's too well guarded, and with there still being some questions related to the king's death, everyone is on high alert. None of the assassins will risk their lives, even for that much gold."

"Double it. Will they risk their lives then?"

The man let out a sharp whistle and shook his head. "Maybe once things calm down. If the guard relaxes some."

"But not now."

"I'm afraid not, but" he hesitated, "There is one man who could do it."

"Who?" Hope resurfaced.

"The Beast, the one you hired to kill Lady Isabella."

Nixa groaned and shot the man an angry glare. "And do you know where to find him?"

"Well," the man raised his hands helplessly. "Not really."

"No. No one does. He disappeared shortly after he *neglected* to kill Lady Isa for me."

"She's not dead?" the man asked in surprise.

Nixa shrugged. "Rumor has it that she's now a princess in the elves' Winter Kingdom. And I would not be surprised if her husband, the scarred prince, was not our missing assassin."

The man's eyes widened in shock. "No."

"Yes," Nixa said with a tilt of her head.

"If that's true, you're right; he won't help."

They stood in silence for an uncomfortable moment.

"Is there nothing you can do?"

"Give it a month or two. Once things relax, I'm sure I'll be able to find someone to take care of it."

Nixa growled and stormed out of the cottage. "A month or two will be too late," she said as she slammed the rickety door behind her.

Nixa felt the weight of the crowd in the council chambers as if it were a physical presence in the room. They were all there: the high counselors, the lords and ladies. Each of them vied for the attention of the queen, who sat on the throne at the head of the room. Nixa waited patiently in her place at the bottom of the dais, though she could feel her heart pounding faster and faster in her chest. Finally, Queen Stelia spoke.

"Thank you all for coming. I know there has been some unrest since the untimely death of our beloved monarch." A tear slid down her face, and she demurely wiped it away. "He was a good and benevolent king, loved by all, and we will miss him terribly." She held up her hand. "There is always some concern when a beloved king's reign ends. People wonder if things will change— if the new king will be as kind and generous. Have no fear. My son, Prince Edward, will be the new ruler of this kingdom as soon as he comes of age. In the meantime, I will assume command in his place, and we will rule with the same fairness and justice that you have enjoyed throughout the previous king's reign."

A flurry of murmurs swept through the chamber. Nixa clenched her fists and stepped forward.

"Stepmother," she said, her voice ringing in the now-hushed chamber. "Since you were not born into royalty as I was, you may not be aware that I am, actually, the rightful heir to the throne. I am the firstborn child of King Reginald, and it is my birthright to rule this kingdom."

The queen bristled at this insult to her intelligence, and a few council members began to whisper, their words like angry wasps buzzing. Nixa held her ground, her voice unwavering.

4

"My claim is legitimate, and I demand that you honor it."

The queen eyed her coldly. "You may have some claim to the throne, Nixa, but you are a lady. Penningdon has only ever had men rule the kingdom. My son is the legal heir to the throne."

"That is not true," Nixa said sweetly. Holding her strained smile made her face ache. "While we have never had a queen sitting on the throne without a king by her side, there is no law stating that a female can't rule alone. The law of this land simply states that the monarchy must pass to the firstborn child. I am the firstborn child; therefore, I am the rightful heir."

The murmurs grew louder as the councilors began to argue amongst themselves, their voices rising in protest. Nixa held her ground, her gaze never leaving the queen.

Finally, the council chairman held up his hand for silence. "This matter requires further investigation," he said, his voice booming in the stillness. "We will look into it and decide. Until then, Queen Stelia will remain as regent."

The council members nodded in agreement, and the room began to clear out. Nixa let out a relieved sigh and allowed herself a small smile of triumph before turning to leave. She had stated her claim, and now it was up to the council chairperson to investigate and make a ruling. Not that she believed they would rule in her favor, not with the queen having control over so many of them, but at least it had bought her some time. If she could keep a final decision from being made until she found an assassin who would take care of the queen for her, her path would be much easier. After all, no one was likely to argue with her taking the throne when her little brother was all who stood in her way.

The Ogre King of Kelgrod sat at a large wooden desk in his dark, windowless office, finishing up a report. A soft blue light orb floated overhead, casting shadows across the bookshelves and the scattered stacks of paper, scrolls of parchment, and leather-bound tomes that populated the area. A light whisper of sound alerted him to the entrance of the spy he had been expecting. He turned his head and watched as the secret door in the bookcase swung open, and the man slunk into the room.

The small, wiry half-ogre appeared relatively puny kneeling before the tall, broad-shouldered ogre king. His half-human physique served him well in his occupation, but he always felt inferior in the presence of pure-blooded ogres. His king had never treated him poorly, though; on the contrary, King Vrag appreciated the advantage his appearance gave him when infiltrating human communities.

"What news?" Vrag leaned forward in anticipation, his hands grasping the arms of his chair and fists clenching tightly. He loomed over the small spy, a dark figure with dark eyes and a fierce expression etched onto his face.

"Her forces are setting up camps along the edge of the forest, and there are rumors that she has made a deal with the dwarves to run training exercises near their southern border. She doesn't seem to be attempting to hide her movements, either."

"That's rather bold of her," the king said. His mouth thinned into a tight line, and his body stiffened, unmoving.

The spy remained kneeling, head down. "I believe," he said hesitantly, "that she hopes her openness will make everyone think her actions are innocent. She has an excuse for them, and she knows that if she tries to hide her movements, someone will most likely see anyway. It would look worse for her if she tried to be sneaky about it."

"What is her excuse?"

"She claims that her men need the experience of fighting in the mountain terrain in case the problems with the goblins move south."

King Vrag snorted. "And her reasons for being in the forest?"

"Goblins like forested areas too."

"Elven forests. They wouldn't bother with human territory, especially not so close to us." The ogre stood and crossed his powerful arms over his broad chest. He walked over to the wall and studied the map that hung there, his dusky gray skin blending into the shadows.

"What of the girl?"

"There is talk that she is planning on fighting for the throne. One of my contacts reported that she stated her claim at the last council meeting. The council is currently deliberating, though it's unlikely that their decision will hold any weight. The queen has strong support from many powerful people in the aristocracy and the military, and she is not one to lightly relinquish such power. There is little doubt that a civil war will ensue if the princess tries to take the throne, no matter what the council decides."

Vrag stared down at the little man. "And do you trust this news?"

The spy squirmed slightly from his position on the floor, bowing his head again. "I do, Your Majesty. The information could have been planted to throw us off, but I doubt it. I have reason to trust my contacts."

The king watched him for a moment longer as he shifted uneasily on his knee. Finally, the large ogre nodded and strode back to his desk.

"Very well. Keep an eye on the situation and report to me if there are any developments."

"Yes, Your Majesty." The spy rose and slipped back through the bookshelf door.

King Vrag rested his head in his hands, his elbows on his desk. That human queen had wanted his kingdom since she first married King Reginald of Penningdon and learned of the wealth of gemstones in the ogre caves. Thankfully, her king had curbed her ambition by insisting that war with the much larger and more skilled immortals would be foolish, especially since it would be next to impossible for her troops to infiltrate their underground city. However, now that the voice of reason in their kingdom was dead, it seemed that her determination was revived.

What was she thinking? Her men would never be able to sneak into the city. Their eyesight wasn't keen enough to navigate the tunnels without some light source, and light sources could be seen from a distance. Easily. And if they couldn't sneak in, they wouldn't make it far before someone challenged them. No matter how skilled, human warriors stood no chance at close combat against ogre warriors, not in the small confines of their cave tunnels.

Either the woman was a complete idiot, or she had some hidden advantage. And he did not believe she was an idiot. So, what was it? What made her so confident that she could pull off this impossible task? Hopefully, his network of spies would come up with something. In the meantime, he had other business that required his attention. Pushing those thoughts from his mind, Vrag once again focused on the report in front of him.

Nix paced angrily in her chambers, her black ball gown swooshing annoyingly against her legs. As inappropriate as it was to have a ball so soon after the king's death, her brother's birthday celebration might be just what she needed. The entire court would be there. They couldn't refuse since the ball was declared to be both a celebration of the late king's life and a celebration of the future king's health. To refuse would seem disloyal.

Nixa snorted as she paced past her mirror. Making it a "black and white" ball was a smart touch since the mourning period had not yet passed. She stopped and admired herself, running her hands down her silk dress. She had always looked good in black, and she needed to look her best tonight if she had any hope of winning over the local nobility. She needed support from the rich and titled if she were to succeed.

Her stepmother had had years to ingratiate herself with everyone of importance, while Nixa had never even considered the need. She had always assumed that she would be queen when her father died. It had never crossed her mind that she wouldn't, not until she saw the look exchanged between that woman and her half-brother the day the king passed. Then, she knew. She understood what they had planned. She only hated that she hadn't thought of it sooner.

But she was thinking of it now. If she couldn't get anyone to kill the queen in time, she would have to win over her supporters. Luckily, most of the power in the kingdom belonged to the aristocratic old men. As a beautiful young princess, she might be able to sway them to her side if she was clever. Nixa tucked a stray black curl back into her updo and gave her image a final glance. Her ruby-red lips turned up into a beguiling smile, a sharp but pleasing contrast to her white, porcelain skin. Perfect.

Striding down the castle corridors, she focused on corralling her anger. The solid stone surrounding her grounded her. The lights and shadows dancing along beside her were companions encouraging her and supporting her in her chosen path. She could do this.

As she reached the ballroom doors, she ignored the guards stationed on each side. They were only minions. She needed to focus on the people in charge. Taking a deep breath, she pasted a smile on her face and nodded for them to open the doors.

Nixa was late. Purposely. The ball was already in full swing when she arrived. She stood at the entrance, looking out over the grandeur of the ballroom. Vibrant music filled the space, and the guests, in their elegant formalwear, swirled around on the dance floor.

She had bribed one of the musicians to make sure that her entrance was noticed by all. He did not disappoint. As soon as she appeared on the balcony at the top of the stairs, the music ceased. One glance showed that the musicians all stared at her, and the eyes of the entire assembly followed suit. In the silence, the herald announced her.

"Her Royal Highness, Princess Nix Alba Pulchritudo Canaveri."

Nixa's eyes found her stepmother. The queen stood in the middle of the ballroom talking to Lord Frederick Creasy, the Duke of Middleton, one of the most powerful men in the kingdom. Excellent, he would make a perfect first target.

Nixa glided elegantly down the stairs, her back straight and head high. She looked the image of a perfect princess. A perfect queen. When she reached the ballroom floor, the musicians started playing again, and the dancers resumed dancing. Nixa floated across the floor to her stepmother. After a shallow curtsey to the queen, too shallow to be entirely proper, she turned to the duke. Without another glance at her stepmother, she held out her hand to him.

"May I have this dance, Your Grace?"

Just the briefest flash of surprise swept across his face to be quickly replaced with a knowing smirk. He was no fool. The game was on. With a bow, he led her into the dance.

Nixa continued her scheme all evening, approaching every man the queen spoke with and asking them to dance. None refused. In this manner, she gradually ate away at the queen's peace of mind.

Queen Stelia steadily grew more and more frazzled and irate as the night progressed, but Nixa remained friendly and charming. She spoke to everyone of importance. She danced with all the influential men. She had never been so charismatic. And by the end of the night, she had never been so exhausted, but if this worked, it would be worth it.

The ball began to wind down, and most people had already drifted off to their chambers or homes when Nixa decided she could finally rest. As she headed back toward the staircase to leave the stuffy ballroom, Lord Creasy approached her and stopped her.

"I admire your effort, princess," he said with a bow, "but perhaps you should use a bit of circumspection. The queen is not a gentle, passive woman. You will face consequences if you do not exercise more caution." Without another word, the duke turned and left.

All the adrenaline and euphoria she had experienced throughout her successful endeavor that evening suddenly vanished as if it had never existed. She felt physically and emotionally drained. Tears welled up in her eyes. She wouldn't break down there. She had to make it to her room.

The smile on her face felt heavy and awkward, but it was the best she could do. She glided out of the ballroom a little less elegantly than she had entered and rushed down the corridor at a pace that was not quite as graceful as would be befitting a queen. The shadows dancing along the corridor following her passage appeared more sinister than before. At least she didn't disgrace herself.

She held on until she made it to her chamber. She held on until her maid had taken down her hair and helped her dress for bed. The moment her door closed, and she was finally alone, she threw herself across her bed and let the sobs come and the tears fall.

# Chapter 2

L ate the following day, Nixa awoke to the muffled sounds of a banging on her outer chamber door and the shuffling of her maid's feet as she rushed to answer it. She raised her hand to her head in a desperate attempt to prevent the headache that was threatening to take over.

She lay there and waited, watching the thin beams of sunlight that squeezed through the curtain dance along the wall. A moment later, her maid knocked timidly on her bedroom door. With a groan, Nixa bid her enter.

"It's a summons from the queen regent, Your Highness."

Suddenly, Nixa was wide awake. Her reckoning had come. Her chest tightened, and her breath seemed to freeze in her lungs; each inhale and exhale came only with great effort. Lord Creasy was right. What had she been thinking? She eased out of bed, keeping up the appearance of a confidence she didn't feel, her head throbbing now.

"Where am I to meet her?"

"In the throne room."

The throne room was good. It represented a position of power for her stepmother since she would undoubtedly be seated on her throne, but it also gave Nixa an advantage. The entire court would attend such a summons. They had witnessed her poise last night, and they had seen the queen's frustration and anger. She had not hidden it well. If her stepmother tried to punish her in any way, it would be recognized exactly for what it was: the revenge of a petty woman, one who didn't deserve to be a queen.

"Bring me the deep burgundy morning gown, please, Greta."

Nixa would face the court in her most regal, yet proper, gown. She would exemplify elegance and make her stepmother appear worse by contrast. Nixa ran various conversations through her head as Greta pinned up her hair.

She didn't know what excuse the queen would use to explain her summons, so she would have to be prepared for any eventuality. She would accuse her of some misconduct. She had no doubt Stelia would find some excuse to punish her, to make her look guilty of something before the court. She would attempt to undo any progress Nixa had made the previous night. By the time she was dressed and ready, she felt confident she could handle any accusation the queen used.

Nixa strolled down the corridor with poise, her chin held high and her back straight. Her heart pounding in her chest. She was calm and composed on the outside, but inside, she could feel a storm of emotions brewing. She reached the heavy double doors, and two guards swung them open as she stepped forward. Her gaze fell on the entire court assembled before her.

Nixa took a deep breath and squared her shoulders. She would need to make a good show of this. She must maintain her composure, no matter how angry or hurt she felt inside. She glided through the doors, pretending each step was part of some carefully choreographed dance instead of a march to her execution.

The conversation between courtiers quieted as she made her way across the room, and they all stilled and watched her pass. But Nixa didn't notice them. Her eyes were glued on the queen sitting on the king's throne as if she belonged there.

Suddenly, Queen Stelia left her seat and came toward Nixa with arms opened wide. Nixa froze as her stepmother approached her and enfolded her in a hug. She had not prepared for this scenario. Her eyes frantically roamed the court while the woman held her tightly.

Had something happened? All the courtiers stood around the room, pleased, sympathetic expressions on their faces. All except Lord Creasy. His eyes met hers, and suddenly, she understood. This game she had started with the queen at the ball, this was her stepmother's move. She would be a worthy opponent. But where was this emotional display going? What was her purpose?

Sniffing, Queen Stelia pulled away from the princess. She held her shoulders and looked her straight in the eyes. For a split second, Nixa saw genuine hatred in those eyes, but then it was gone.

"I visited your father's grave this morning." She sniffed dramatically. "I miss him so much, and I know you do too. I felt his presence there strongly, and he seemed so sad. I want to do more to honor him, to show him how much we still care."

Okay, this conversation was strange, but she could play along.

"I would love that, stepmother," she replied with an equally fake smile. The queen's grin faltered momentarily as if she hadn't expected such a ready agreement, but it returned immediately with a vengeance.

"How do you suggest we accomplish that?" Nixa asked. She realized her error as soon as the question left her mouth. Stelia was in charge of this conversation. She had a plan, and Nixa had just fallen into her trap.

"You know how your father loved the rare purple danneion flowers?"

Nixa knew no such thing. Her father had never cared for flowers at all. They were beneath his notice as most beautiful but useless things were. When she didn't reply, the queen continued.

"My huntsman has told me of a spot in the forest where they grow. Can you imagine?" Her fake excitement began to grate on Nixa's nerves, but she patiently waited to see where this went.

"I think it would mean so much to your father if you were to pick some with your own hands and plant them on his grave." The queen squeezed Nixa's arms, where she still held her. "You can look at this as a little quest, and my huntsman will accompany you. Wouldn't that be a nice thing to do for your father? To show him how much you loved him?"

Nixa's eyes shot to Lord Creasy in the corner. He pressed his lips together and shook his head. So, this was it. She was going to lure her into the forest and do what? Kill her? Possibly. Most likely.

She was trapped. Standing here before the entire court, she couldn't deny the request. She would appear as the worst sort of person, someone who wouldn't do such a small thing to show her love for their late king, for her father.

With a smile that looked more like a grimace, Nixa pulled her stepmother into another embrace. She squeezed her tightly, viciously. She made sure Stelia understood that she wasn't fooled.

"Of course, Stepmother. Nothing would make me happier. I'll go tomorrow." She needed time to plan, to contact some people.

"Nonsense, my dear. There's no time like the present. Go now. I'll take care of any little matters that might need your attention today. The sooner you begin, the sooner we can honor your father properly."

With a tight-lipped nod, Nixa turned and swept out of the room. She heard the steps of the huntsman following her, but she didn't look back. When she moved past the castle's main entrance, the huntsman stepped in front of her. "We can exit here, Your Highness," he said with a slight bow.

She glared at the man but was still mindful of the open doors to the throne room and all the people inside, some of whom were watching their progress.

"I must change my gown before going on such a quest." She held out the wide skirt of her silk dress. "You don't expect me to wear this while trekking through the forest, do you?"

The man shot a quick look back into the throne room before replying.

"Of course not, Your Highness." He waved his hand, indicating that she should lead the way. Nixa swept her skirts with a flourish as she continued to her rooms.

She slammed her chamber door in the huntsman's face and called for Greta. Quickly changing into her plainest, sturdiest gown, she had the maid pack a small bag for her. She pulled the pins from her hair and twisted it into a simple braid.

Greta didn't ask any questions. Undoubtedly, the servants had already been discussing the situation. She probably knew more about what was happening than Nixa did. But she trusted her lady's maid. She didn't, however, trust the huntsman. Nixa pulled her dagger out of her dresser drawer and stuck it in her boot. Greta handed her the small bag, and she tied it up under her skirts.

"I might not be back for a while, Greta," she said.

"I understand, Princess."

Nixa paused when she saw tears gathering in her maid's eyes. She hugged her quickly when the huntsman knocked on the door.

"We need to hurry, Your Highness. I fear we will have a storm coming through before long."

Nixa shot a quick glance out the window at the bright, sunny, cloudless sky. She sighed as she faced Greta again.

"Take care of yourself. I'll try to get back as soon as I safely can."

"Be careful, Princess."

Nixa nodded and, with a deep breath, turned to the door.

"The queen has ordered the death of the princess."

Once again, the spy, Number One, knelt before the ogre king, this time in his chambers. Vrag sat at his table, surrounded by paperwork, while eating a rushed supper.

He stared into the flames burning in the fireplace on the side wall.

"How have the people responded?"

"They don't know. She disguised the execution as a quest for the princess to show her love for her late father. The queen's huntsman is to accompany her. He will complete the task once they are far enough from the kingdom."

The ogre king nodded and turned back to his plate. He slowly chewed as he thought.

"Who do you have following them?"

"Number Eight."

Another nod. "Any more movement of their troops?"

"No, Your Majesty, at least not much. They have settled into their new posts. A trickle of additional men arrive at each location daily, but not enough to cause comment."

"But enough to add up over time and make a difference in a war?"

"Yes, Your Majesty."

"Do you have numbers?"

"Not yet. Their movements have appeared rather unorganized and irregular, making it difficult to count. But Number Five is at the mountain location, and Number Three is in the forest now. They should have more information soon."

"Let me know as soon as you find out."

With a nod, the spy left. Vrag cut off a piece of meat and bit into it, savoring the flavors that danced across his tongue. *What is that ridiculous human hiding?* he thought. *What makes her so confident that she can defeat me? Or is she the fool she appears to be?* He must be ready for anything.

Rising from his seat, he walked over to the wall and pulled the cord hanging down from the ceiling. Then, he returned to the table and continued his meal. Only a few moments later, a servant entered the room.

"You rang, Your Majesty."

"Find Captain Uenk. We have matters to discuss."

Nixa followed the huntsman deep into the forest. She could feel the weight of the dagger in her boot with every step. Logically, she knew that even with her dagger, she stood little chance of survival if the man with her decided to attack. She was not skilled with the weapon even though she knew a few moves. Emotionally, she took some comfort from the heavy metal pressing against her leg.

She felt a pit grow in her stomach as they walked without speaking. The silence between them swelled thick and heavy with tension. Nixa strained to keep up with the man, weaving through the trees and underbrush, desperate to remember a single landmark that would map her escape.

She needed to remember how to return to the castle, but the huntsman took her down so many twists and turns in the thick forest that she quickly lost her sense of direction. At the edge of a small clearing filled with wildflowers, the man stopped so suddenly that she almost collided with him as he spun to face her. His steely gaze attacked her, penetrating through every defense she had built up until her heart was racing and her knees quaking.

"You've brought me out here to kill me, haven't you?" she asked with a gulp.

He pinned her with a pair of cold eyes. "Those were my instructions, yes."

Nixa considered, not for the first time, trying to run away, but she discarded the idea just as she had all the other times it had invaded her mind. She was utterly lost, and despite the weapon in her boot, she knew she had no chance in the forest alone at night. She had heard stories about the dangerous animals that lived there. Besides, he was a huntsman. He knew these woods. He could easily find her wherever she ran.

"Would it accomplish anything if I attempted to bribe you?"

"No."

"What about threats? I'm sure Lord Creasy will be suspicious of my sudden demise."

"No."

"Power? If I become queen, I can give you anything you want."

"No."

Nixa's mind raced. How could she convince this man to spare her life? The irony of her situation didn't escape her. She wondered if this was what Lady Isa had been thinking when she faced the assassin Nixa had recently sent after her. Perhaps she deserved this. Yes. She definitely deserved this.

The huntsman stood there silently watching her as these recriminations rushed through her head.

"I am not going to kill you," he said, interrupting her thoughts.

"What?" Nixa asked, surprised. "Why not?"

"Loyalty. I was loyal to your father. He was a good king, and I refuse to get involved in this conflict between his wife and daughter. Whoever becomes the next queen or king, I will be loyal to them, but I will not become involved, by my actions, in contributing to any specific outcome."

Nixa released a breath she hadn't even realized she was holding.

The man held her gaze intently. "I will offer you this advice, though: consider carefully before you make a move against the queen regent. She has the full support of the military, the support of the majority of the council, and the support of the aristocracy and the city's merchants. You have none of those. She also has a reputation as a good ruler. Your reputation is that of a spoiled princess."

Nixa narrowed her eyes at that comment.

"Forgive my bluntness, Your Highness. I only wish to speak the truth. If you pursue your attempt to take the throne, much blood will be shed, the kingdom will be torn, and you will die either in battle or at the hand of an assassin. You cannot win this war. I advise you to forget your past, move on with your life, and disappear. If you don't, when the queen realizes I didn't follow her orders, she will send someone else after you. She will have you dead before you can gather support to oppose her." With a quick bow, he added, "I wish you luck with your future," and disappeared into the surrounding trees.

Nixa stood stunned, staring in the direction the huntsman had vanished. The wind stirred through the branches. Birds sang in the trees. Everything around her exuded peace and tranquility. But the calm twirling around her didn't penetrate the chaos raging inside.

She fell to her knees and then sat down on the dried leaves covering the forest floor. Her whole world was collapsing, crashing down around her in the midst of this serene oasis. Such a strange sensation, the chaos mixed with the peace.

The huntsman was right. She had been a fool, living her life just for pleasure all these years. She had let her pride and vanity drive all her actions, focusing only on making conquests of all the handsome men she encountered. And she had ignored everyone who didn't fit into that category. She had no contacts, no supporters. Other than the occasional servant she could bribe for little tasks and her faithful Greta, she had no one she could count on to help her in her time of need.

What could she do? If she were going to attempt to take back the kingdom, how could she accomplish it? Who would help her?

Despair washed over her as the realization of the true helplessness of her situation fully hit her. Nothing. She could do nothing. If she went to a neighboring kingdom and somehow convinced them to assist in her coup, they would require a high price for their support. Too high, most likely.

The huntsman was right. There would be a war. Hundreds, if not thousands, of people would die. She might die. Then, the best she could hope for would be to rule in name only and owe allegiance to another country.

Nixa's face fell into her hands as her sobs overwhelmed her. She grieved the loss of her dreams. She had always known she would be queen someday. When she thought of her future, that is the image that always played across her imagination.

That future, those dreams, died then and there, and she mourned their passing. She mourned them more than she had mourned the death of her father.

Not only that but if she wanted to escape the queen, the huntsman was right, she would have to hide. She would need to change her identity. She could no longer be Princess Nixa. Her sobs gained intensity at the additional loss of her self. She mourned the loss of her name, her person. The only self she had ever known also died.

She sat there, huddled on the forest floor for what felt like hours, what felt like seconds. Her whole life changed in the middle of those woods, and she grew emotionally. She understood herself better. She understood her weaknesses and where she had gone astray. She knew there was no going back. She did not want to go back, not to the person she had been. When her tears finally dried, she rose to her feet a stronger, wiser woman.

Nixa scanned the surrounding forest. She had no idea where she was, but that didn't matter since she no longer cared where she went. She only knew that she didn't want to return to the castle. She would find a small village somewhere and get a job. This thought made her pause. How would she earn a living? She didn't know how to do anything. She took a deep breath and straightened her back. She would figure it out.

She began walking slowly, letting her feet take the lead. She was surrounded by so much beauty. The trees towered around her, and the sunlight filtered through the branches, making beautiful patterns on the forest floor.

She passed a babbling stream that sparkled in the light, and she stopped, mesmerized by its tranquility. The serenity of the nature around her calmed her. It felt like balm to her wounded soul. Peace enveloped her. The sun shone through the canopy of trees above, and she smiled at the beauty of it all.

The deeper into the forest she ventured, the more mysterious it became, but she wasn't afraid. Ancient trees loomed around her, and their branches seemed to whisper secrets as they brushed against each other in the wind. All sense of time escaped Nixa as she immersed herself in this world.

# *Chapter 3*

Nixa's stomach had growled several times, and the shadows had lengthened when she finally stumbled into a small glade. Tall trees surrounded it, forming a protective barrier from the outside world. In the center sat a humble cabin made of logs and stones. A thin trail of smoke drifted from the chimney, disappearing into the gray sky, and curtains hanging in its open windows waved lightly in the breeze.

Nixa hesitated before she left the tree line. She couldn't help but remember the last house, sitting in the middle of a clearing, that she had entered. She shook the thought from her mind. She was a different person now. She would be a different person now.

She wished she could remain in the forest forever. She didn't think she was ready to engage with people again. She feared she would lose the tranquility she had found in the woods. But logic asserted itself. She couldn't survive out here on her own. She didn't even know how to start a fire, let alone how to find anything to cook over it. With a deep breath, she approached the cottage and knocked.

The door opened slowly, and an older dwarf appeared, his shoulder-length gray hair not quite matching his short, neatly trimmed black beard. He looked her up and down, his face wrinkled in scrutiny. Nixa felt herself shrinking under his gaze. Maybe this was a mistake. She was about to turn away when the dwarf finally spoke.

"What do you want?" he asked gruffly.

Nixa took a deep breath before she answered, her voice soft but sure, "I need something to eat and a place to stay."

The dwarf studied her for a long moment before finally nodding his head in acquiescence. "We can help you," he said, "if you agree to cook for us and do some cleaning."

"I will be glad to try," she replied hesitantly, "but I feel like I should warn you that I don't have any experience with either."

The dwarf narrowed his eyes at her. "Well, I suppose you can learn." He stood back for her to enter.

Several other dwarves sat around a large table in the middle of the room. Wooden beams crisscrossed the ceiling, and the crackling of the fire and bubbling of something in a pot blended into a cozy background hum. The rustic atmosphere and the warm glow of the fire wrapped around her like a thick blanket.

Nixa's eyes turned to the table as the aroma of roasted meat and freshly baked bread assaulted her senses. Her stomach growled again, reminding her that she hadn't had anything to eat that day.

"Hello," she said, lowering herself into the chair that one of the dwarves moved to the table for her.

They all eyed her warily, but no one replied.

"I'm...Mary." Nixa glanced around the table nervously as they all stared at her. The incredulity lining their faces told her they didn't believe her assumed name, at least most of them.

One of the dwarves, sitting across from her, stared at her with a lopsided grin. "You're pretty," he said with a blush. His wide eyes, in his childlike face, watched her adoringly.

Nixa had been called beautiful, gorgeous, stunning, and other similar things her entire life. She bristled a little at the insult of being considered merely pretty, but then she remembered that her vanity was partially to blame for her being in this mess. She swallowed her frustration and examined the man in front of her. His smile appeared genuine, and he clearly meant his statement as a compliment. She decided to take it as such and smiled back at him.

The youngest dwarf at the table leaned forward. His bright blue eyes twinkled in the firelight, and Nixa felt herself relax a bit.

"Hi, Mary," he said, "I'm Garroth. It's nice to meet you." He gestured to the other dwarves around the table, "These are my brothers: Durfal, Thondrak, Ubril, Varfid, Brulin, and Harnic." He pointed lastly to the one who had complimented her, and the grin on his face spread at the introduction.

Some of them nodded at her, while others just grumbled in response. After everyone had been introduced, Brulin, the one who had opened the door to her, motioned towards the feast on the table and said kindly, "Let's eat!"

Nixa chided herself on how she had immediately forgotten all their names. If she was trying to change and be more considerate and aware of ordinary people, she wasn't off to a good start. She'd have to make a special effort to remember their names the next time she heard them.

She eagerly helped herself to some food before settling into a hesitant conversation with her new companions.

As the days passed into weeks, Nixa slowly started to feel more at home at the cabin. She learned how to chop wood for the fire, sweep up dirt on the hardwood floors, and even make bread from scratch. At first, she was clumsy about it all, and many times, she bristled at their expectations of her performing such lowly tasks. She was a princess, after all. But at those times, she had only to look around at the humble surroundings to remind herself that she was a princess no longer. Unless... But, no. She was a princess no longer.

As time passed, she got better at the various jobs and felt more comfortable in her new role. She quickly grew accustomed to the dwarves' routines, cooking meals for them in the mornings before helping tidy around the house. In exchange, they taught her how to start a fire and hunt for food.

It wasn't long before the dwarves began to accept her presence, and soon, she became an integral part of their little family. Garroth, especially, took it upon himself to teach her the many secrets of the forest: what plants were edible, which animals should be avoided, and, more importantly, how to blend in with nature so that she could effectively hide when necessary. They spent lots of time hunting together, enjoying the outdoors and exploring nature.

As Nixa's confidence grew, she found herself reveling in her newfound freedom, and she often stayed out late on long hikes in the forest. One day, she discovered a hidden waterfall at the edge of a cliff and sat on the banks of the stream, watching the water cascade down. She loved the peace and solitude found here but couldn't deny that part of her longed for the life she had left behind.

She missed the excitement and energy that filled the air of the large city. The palpable spark that permeated everything there. The castle exuded life. The forest, while she loved it, seemed lacking in comparison to her memories. She needed this time to rest and to learn, but she knew she couldn't stay forever. She would eventually have to move on. But where?

*Should* she try to retake the kingdom, no matter how foolish it seemed, or should she take the wiser course and follow the huntsman's advice? If so, where could she go? She was learning some skills, but the pride she hadn't entirely conquered yet wouldn't let her even entertain the idea of working as a maid in a major city.

She was young and beautiful. She could probably still find some rich man to marry her, even if she had to pretend to be poor. But that wasn't what she wanted either, to sell herself to the highest bidder just to have someone to take care of her. It would be exchanging one prison for another.

Nixa heaved herself off the forest floor. She cast one last glance at the beautiful waterfall and turned to head back to the cottage.

The forest was alive with chirping birds, buzzing insects, and rustling leaves. She walked past a patch of wild blueberries she had picked earlier and smiled as she noticed mushrooms growing in a shady corner. Nature was bountiful, and Nixa realized how lucky she was to have been able to experience it firsthand. Knowing what she did about plants and animals now, she felt confident that if it became necessary, she could survive out here in the woods on her own.

No, Nixa decided, whatever path she chose for herself from now on, it would involve other people and most likely involve taking risks. She could see no other way forward than to take life into her own hands. She just had to decide what that life would look like.

King Vrag silently approached Number Eight as he stood hidden in the trees, watching the girl by the waterfall.

"Has she had contact with anyone?" he whispered. Human ears were so weak he had no concern that the girl would hear them.

"No. I stay with her all the time she's outside, and Number Nine is watching the dwarves. We would have seen if anyone had attempted anything."

"I just checked in with Number Nine. One of the dwarves is headed to the village. Follow him. I'll stay here until a replacement arrives."

The ogre spy cast a curious glance at his king. While it wasn't unusual for a king to meet with troops or spies out in the field, it was odd that he would volunteer to take on the surveillance task by himself. And this was not the first time that King Vrag had done so. Number Eight just nodded and disappeared into the forest.

Vrag leaned against a tree and crossed his thick arms, gazing, puzzled, at the tiny human female sitting so near.

Something about her fascinated him, but he couldn't figure out what. She was very beautiful, for a human, of course. There was no denying that, but that couldn't be the problem because she *was* a human. And ogres didn't think of humans that way.

No, it must be her spirit. Her determination. He liked that. He had watched her several times since she had come to live with the dwarves. A fact that perplexed his spy network. During that time, he had seen her transform from a helpless, weak, ignorant human girl to a slightly less helpless, weak, ignorant human girl.

She had, perhaps, learned as much as she could about the forest surrounding her, given her lack of strength and her dull human senses. What struck him the most, though, was that she hadn't given up, even when things got difficult. When she had to chop the wood or follow faint animal tracks, she never gave up. She'd built up her muscles as much as she could, honed her senses as much as possible, and learned all about the animals and the fruits and herbs that grew in the area, as much as her small human brain could hold. Yes, he admired her spirit. She would make a good pet. A pretty pet.

He considered the idea as he stood there watching her weave a crown out of flowers. If this whole thing ended up being a trick by the queen to get the princess close enough to spy on them, capturing her and taking her into the underground kingdom would be a mistake. However, if that were the case, it had been planned out very well, especially since she had been cut off from all communication with the castle ever since she left the huntsman.

On the other hand, if she really were hiding from the queen, she would be found soon. The soldiers grew increasingly bold as they gradually moved closer and closer to Kelgrod Mountains. He would hate to see her killed by her stepmother. However, if she turned out to be a spy, he would kill her himself.

No, it was too soon. He had time. The queen was still being cautious. She wouldn't move her troops this close to the ogre mountains for at least a few more weeks. He would continue to watch the girl. It was only a matter of time before he discovered the truth.

As Nixa approached the cottage after spending another beautiful day roaming the woods, she could tell immediately that something was wrong. The door stood open, and Durfal and Ubril paced outside. Their heads shot in her direction as she approached.

"Here she is," Durfal yelled into the house. The rest of the brothers hurried out.

"Are you alright?" asked Garroth.

Nixa laughed nervously. "Of course I am. What's going on."

The dwarves exchanged glances.

"I just got back from the village," Brulin said. "Rumor has it that the princess isn't dead after all."

"Princess Nixa?" Nixa asked innocently.

Burlin gave her a hard look. "Yes, Princess Nixa. There is talk that the queen is searching for her. She claims she wants to rescue her from her kidnappers, but no one believes that. There's no way the princess was kidnapped. The queen searches for her so she can dispose of her. She is the only real threat to her throne, after all."

"Hmm, that's interesting," said Nixa, glancing nonchalantly at her fingernails.

"We know who you are," Ubril said.

Nixa looked at them. These men, who had become like family to her over the last few weeks, now glared at her, hands on hips, as if daring her to deny it. Nixa sighed.

"Very well, I admit it. What do you think I should do now?"

"Well, you certainly can't keep wandering around the forest like you've been," said Garroth.

"And you can't stay here alone at the cottage while we're working in the mines, either," added Brulin.

Durfal and the others nodded in agreement. "You will have to stay with us at all times so we can look out for you."

Nixa gave them a weak smile. She knew they were only trying to protect her, but her cage grew tighter with those words and threatened to strangle her completely.

Nixa sat, exhausted, on a boulder inside the mine. She had insisted on working with the dwarves instead of just sitting and watching them all day, but she hadn't realized how much strength was required to break through the hard walls of the cave. They made it look so easy.

The klink, klink of the dwarves' pickaxes echoed in the tall space as they tirelessly chipped away at the stone, searching for precious gems. Nixa took a deep breath and glanced around. The cave walls and ceiling dripped with water, and the air was thick with moisture and the smell of damp earth. Nixa couldn't deny that this place, like the forest, had its own mysterious attraction—an attraction rooted in the hidden wonders that lay beneath the surface in this old mine.

Occasionally, one of the dwarves would shout out in delight when they found something, and these moments made everyone around them smile, filling the group with renewed enthusiasm to keep working.

By the time they packed up for home, Nixa was exhausted. She admired their dedication, strength, and skill but couldn't help feeling envious. At least they had a purpose and knew what to expect each day. She felt like she was drifting along without any goal or meaning to her life.

As she had learned the skills of cooking, cleaning, and foraging, Nixa soon picked up the skills required to mine, too. Her arms grew stronger, and she became better at recognizing gems hidden beneath the hard rock surface. Despite this newfound strength and knowledge, Nixa couldn't help but think of herself as an entombed stone—just waiting for some escape from her prison. Refusing to give in to despair, Nixa pushed forward with her new craft until, one day, she found something special—a diamond so perfect that it sparkled like starlight when exposed to even the faintest source of light. This discovery made her heart soar with joy. She knew she would treasure it forever, not only for its beauty but also as a reminder of this time in her life. It also gave her a new sense of hope. Perhaps, even in the dullness of her life when she was trapped in her own cave wall, someone would find her and set her free, too.

One morning, shortly after they had started work for the day, Varfid suddenly cried out as his pickax crashed through the hard surface of the wall. Nixa glanced over at him curiously to see what had happened, but the other dwarves quickly closed ranks around him.

"What is it?" she asked, confused by their strange behavior.

"Oh, nothing to worry about," said Brulin. His voice sounded a bit more strained than usual. They were not good liars, these dwarves, which was a positive quality for a person to have, in her opinion.

"Really?" she stretched the word out, showing her disbelief.

The other dwarves quickly began filling in the hole behind Brulin. He raised his hand, palms up, his voice rising as well.

"Really." He shifted his feet nervously and glanced back over his shoulder.

The other dwarves moved away from the now-sealed hole and picked up their tools.

"I think we've found everything we're going to find in this section," said Ubril.

"Yes."

"I agree."

"That's true."

They responded too quickly, and Nixa could see, just from a glance around, that many more gems lay hidden or even only partially hidden in the surrounding walls. The men kept up a continual stream of chatter as they shepherded her out of that recess and back into the main mining tunnel: everything was fine; there were just better areas they hadn't explored yet; nothing more could be found there; they should try the western line. Even a child wouldn't be fooled by their rapid assertions. Nixa couldn't stop herself from laughing at the absurdity of it all.

"You are terrible liars," she told them.

Garroth winced.

"What is it that you are so determined to hide from me? Surely, you know I can handle it now after all I've learned since I've been here with you."

The men glanced at each other skeptically.

"It's not that we don't think you can handle it. It's just..." Garroth hesitated, not wanting to offend the princess.

"Just what?"

"Well, you can't deny that you have a voracious curiosity," said Thondrak.

"And you don't always have the best self-control," added Ubril.

Nixa blinked rapidly at these accusations. She had thought she'd grown lately with all her introspection and attempts to discover who she was deep down inside. She'd identified many of her failings, but curiosity and a lack of self-control were not issues she had considered. She couldn't argue with their deductions, though.

"Okay, I'll admit to that, but now that I'm aware of those failings in myself, perhaps I'll be able to control them better. What is it that you think I'll be too curious about?"

Still, they hesitated.

"With my insatiable curiosity, you know I'll just find some way to sneak back there and check it out myself if you don't tell me."

That was the wrong thing to say. Brulin and Thondrak huffed into their beards while the others' faces turned to granite.

*Oh, great*, she thought. She'd pushed them too far. Now, they would be stubborn about the whole thing and watch her like a hawk. She'd never find out what the big secret was now. But her time growing up in the castle hadn't been a total waste. She had learned how to deal with people and how to be patient. She would make them let down their guard, and she would find out what the big deal was.

It wasn't so much that she had to know as it was that they didn't want her to know. She still struggled with her pride. She didn't like other people attempting to control her actions. Besides, this was rather exciting. Whatever it was, it brought some joy and adventure back into a life that was increasingly growing too peaceful.

Nixa laughed again in an attempt to ease the protective tension permeating the cave. Luckily, she *was* a good liar.

"Don't worry guys. I'm not that crazy. I trust you. Whatever reason you have that you don't want me to know about what you found, I can respect that. I just wish you trusted me enough to tell me why I can't know.

The dwarves, Garroth in particular, seemed quite abashed at her comment. The young dwarf frowned and shifted his pickaxe to his other shoulder.

"It's not that we don't trust you, Nixa, it's just that...what we found is dangerous, and we don't want you to get hurt."

Nixa had pity on the young man. She decided to let them off the hook. She'd drop the subject and, hopefully, their suspicion as well.

"Okay, then, I believe you. It's dangerous, and I need to stay away from it." She nodded her head to emphasize her words.

They nodded in response, even though most of them didn't seem entirely convinced of her sincerity.

"Come on," she said in an attempt to distract them. "Let's go check out the western tunnel. I heard it was worth exploring." With a grin, she bounded off in that direction, not even allowing herself a glance back at the mysterious, abandoned wall.

# Chapter 4

A week had passed before the dwarves stopped jumping to attention every time she moved in the mines. They had been watching her carefully the entire time they worked underground. They must have found time for a secret meeting at some point because one of them had their eyes on her every moment of the day.

While the others worked, one of them—they rotated the responsibility throughout the day—would sit on a boulder and rest, or stop to get a drink, or walk around examining the walls for places to dig, or some other such nonsense that allowed them to keep her in sight. She would have found it funny if it hadn't been so exasperating. It didn't really bother her to badly, however, because she could wait.

Despite all her other failings, she could be patient when there was something she wanted. And the dwarves must have been right about her because her curiosity was eating her up inside. Of course, that had more to do with them being so determined to keep her away and the incredibly dull state of her current existence than any seriously warped sense of curiosity on her part.

After about a week, their diligence had relaxed somewhat, and she finally felt free to make her move. They had just discovered a particularly rich vein, and everyone was hacking away at it excitedly. Now was her chance.

"I need to step outside for a moment," she said, laying her pick on the ground and taking one of the torches from the wall.

They all glanced back at her suspiciously.

"Durfal can go with you," said Brulin.

Durfal leaned his pick against the wall and brushed his hands down his pants legs.

"No, Durfal can't go with me," said Nixa somewhat desperately.

At their startled glances, she quickly added.

"I need to take care of a private business."

Their stares remained blank and uncomprehending.

"I need to answer the call of nature?"

The men blushed and stammered, none more than Durfal, as he grasped his pick and began chipping away at the wall again. The others quickly followed suit, except for Brulin.

"I don't like you going out by yourself. What if the queen's men are out there somewhere?"

Nixa waved away the idea. "Don't be silly. They have no idea where I am. Besides, I won't be gone long." She grabbed a torch off the wall, turned, and walked away before he could find another excuse to stop her.

"I expect to see several gemstones freed by the time I return," she called back over her shoulder.

Grunts of agreement accompanied her down the tunnel.

She walked quietly, listening for any heavy footsteps following her. Hearing none, she picked up her pace and turned down into the forbidden passage. When she reached the hole, she hurried to remove the pile of stones they had used to cover it.

Peering into the gap, she gasped. It was another tunnel, its walls glistening with moisture and lit with a glow that had no visible source. A narrow path led off into darkness, and the air smelled of something earthy and magical that set her heart racing with excitement. Why had the dwarves been so frightened of her seeing this? Wasn't it just an old mining tunnel?

She glanced around looking for the source of the soft light that spread throughout the passage but couldn't see any explanation for it. No. This wasn't an old mining tunnel. This was something else.

Something different.

Something forbidden.

Whatever it was, she had to discover its secret. The dwarves were just a few tunnels away. What could go wrong? Without another thought, Nixa crawled through the hole and took off down the path, eager to see where it led.

The tunnel twisted and turned, slowly leading her deeper into the mountain. As she walked, Nixa felt a chill in the air that made her shiver despite the heat emanating from her torch. She moved forward cautiously, not wanting to disturb anything that might be lurking in the shadows.

Suddenly, Nixa heard a skittering noise coming from somewhere nearby. She froze mid-step and held her breath as she strained to make out where it came from. But all she could see were small shiftings in the darkness above as if something was running along with her but staying just out of sight.

The tunnel grew darker with each step Nixa took. She held the torch up to get a better look at the walls, but it only illuminated a few feet ahead of her. There *was* something scurrying in the shadows nearby; she just knew it. She shivered as an icy breeze blew through the passage, sending goosebumps along her arms. But still she continued.

The walls seemed to go on forever. Nixa felt like she was walking in a dream as she passed through the dimly lit tunnels. Every now and then, her eyes would catch a flicker of movement from just out of sight in the darkness. She heard more scuttling nearby but never saw more than small fragments of inky blackness darting back and forth.

Nixa felt her breath leave her when she finally reached the end of the tunnel. Before her, stretched an expansive cavern filled with towering stalagmites and glittering gemstones embedded in its walls. A deep blue shimmer ran across its ceiling, emanating from hundreds of glowing orbs clustered above it, all like stars in the night sky. In its center sat a pool of crystal-clear water, reflecting the light above. But most astonishing of all were the buildings that dotted the cavern floor and the enormous castle sitting in their midst. A sprawling city lay below her.

Her mind raced. Could it be a dwarven city? Surely not. The dwarves wouldn't have been so worried about that, and wouldn't they have been living here if it were? Maybe a goblin city? But she had heard that the goblins lived on the other side of the mountains. Ogres? Possibly. The location would fit, but no one had seen the ancient enemies of the humans for centuries. She had once heard her father and stepmother talking about them, but when she had asked him about it later, he had denied they still existed. They were just characters in stories—horrible, frightening characters who would sooner skin a human alive and then eat them than talk to them. A new terror seized her at that thought.

Nixa backed slowly away from the ledge overlooking the city. She had to get out of there and quickly. Suddenly, a loud crack sounded behind her, and Nixa stopped short. She could feel something watching her from the depths of the darkness. Icy tendrils wrapped around her heart, slowly squeezing it shut. Fear seized her, paralyzing her. Maybe she should have listened to the dwarves.

A low, rumbling voice spoke behind her, like granite rubbing against stone.

"What are you doing here?"

A sharp spike dug slightly into her back, sending a shooting pain down her spine. She turned to see two towering ogres with their spears pointed at her. Their leather armor gleamed lightly in the dim glow of her torch, and shining tattoos carved intricate patterns across their faces and down their bare, muscled arms. They were huge. She stood, trembling before them.

"I'm sorry. I didn't mean to intrude." She glanced back down the tunnel. "I stumbled across this tunnel and just wondered where it led. I meant no harm."

She had to crane her neck to see their faces, hovering at least a head and a half above hers. Though their warrior appearance completely terrified her, not to mention the fierce expressions on their faces, they were not as horrible-looking as the stories said. They were quite a bit larger than humans, but their features looked not unlike those of human men.

"Tell it to the captain," said one of the ogres. He removed his spear from her back so she could turn around but immediately used it again to prod her forward down a side passage. Nixa's heart raced as she followed the lead ogre out of the tunnel and down a steep slope into the city. As they moved closer to the cavern floor, the passage opened into a narrow trail lining the side of the cavern wall.

The city loomed larger and larger the nearer they came. Everywhere she looked, structures adorned with colorful banners rose towered the cavern ceiling. The street was busy with merchants hawking their wares and citizens bustling about their daily lives.

She clutched her torch tightly as if it were a lifeline. Just as she had known her dagger would be useless against the huntsmen, she knew that the same dagger, still hidden in her boot, and the torch she carried would be useless as weapons against these great beasts. But just as with the dagger and the huntsman, she took some comfort from the feel of the torch in her hands.

Eventually, they reached a deep crevice filled with winding stairs that led down to a vast open space below them. The air here was thicker, heavy, and hard to breathe. Everything smelled damp and musty as if it hadn't been used in years, but clearly, it had. The bustle of the marketplace could be heard more easily the lower they descended.

Nixa's legs ached by the time they reached the bottom step. Immediately before them stood an immense guard barracks surrounded by a large stone wall that extended outwards in all directions like a fortress. Nixa hesitated as she saw it, but the stab of a spear into her back hurried her along. She resisted the urge to rub the painful spots the impatient, overzealous guard created and obediently entered the foreboding building.

The guards led Nixa down the long hallways of the ogre's barracks, her heart pounding with each step. Torchlight glinted off the stones as they walked, casting an eerie glow over the walls and darkening corners. The farther they went, the more oppressive the atmosphere became until, finally, they reached a large wooden door at the end of one of the corridors. Thick planks reinforced with metal bands identified the intimidating door as one protecting something important. The two additional ogre guards on either side of the entrance supported that idea. They held their spears crossed before them and eyed Nixa fiercely as she approached.

One of the ogres pounded on the door with his spear haft, opening it for them after a gruff voice from within bid them enter. Nixa took a deep breath and cautiously stepped inside.

Massive furniture filled the expansive room, and racks of large deadly weapons stood along the walls. In one corner, a tall desk piled high with books and papers partially blocked an immense bookshelf from view. The sound of someone clearing his throat drew Nixa's gaze to the imposing figure behind the desk. His gaze fixed upon her as she entered. His expression was unreadable but entirely commanding as he leaned forward, waiting to hear why she was there.

"We found her sneaking around in the southern passageway leading into the city, Captain Uenk" said one of her guards.

The captain stared at her curiously, his large head tilted to one side. His pointed ears twitched as if he were listening to her rapidly beating heart.

He leaned forward in his chair and steepled his hands, his elbows resting on his desk.

"Welcome to Kelgrod, Princess Nixa."

Nixa held her breath, her muscles freezing in place as she waited. He knew who she was. Was that a good thing or a bad thing?

"Don't worry," he said, gentling the natural roughness of his voice. "We won't kill you. Yet."

Nixa could only stare at him.

"You see, we don't kill spies here in Kelgrod, at least not until we can have a little talk with them first."

Nixa took a gasping breath. "I'm not a spy," she insisted desperately. "I'm hiding from the queen. She's trying to kill me. I just wanted to escape." She shook her head frantically. "I didn't even mean to come here. I saw the tunnel and simply followed it, wanting to know where it led." Her voice trailed off pitifully at the end. She realized how flimsy her excuse sounded.

"Perhaps," said the captain. "We'll find the truth out after a few conversations."

The way he said that last word sent renewed terror throughout her body. She hadn't realized she could get any more frightened, but the stories she'd heard also mentioned how the ogres tortured humans during their interrogations as well as simply for the fun of it. They would torture them and then eat them. Oh, why hadn't she listened to the dwarves?

The captain addressed the guards. "Send a message to the king and escort our guest to one of our guest rooms below."

"Wait, please!" cried the princess, but the captain waved them away. A guard roughly grabbed her arm and pulled her along behind him. Nixa stumbled, trying to keep up with his long strides. He didn't even slow. He just dragged her on as if he hadn't even noticed she'd fallen. She tried to scramble to her feet, and that motion finally captured his attention. He paused for only a moment to allow her to regain her footing. He still didn't slow, however, as he continued down the hallway, and she had to practically run to keep up with him.

Eventually, they reached a door with two large metal bars across it. With a grunt, the guard forced it open and dragged Nixa down the dimly lit stairs into a dark dungeon.

It smelled of urine and decay. He threw her into one of the cold, damp cells that lined both sides of the hallway, then slammed the door shut behind him and locked it with a heavy clunk.

Nixa's fear had reached its peak as she surveyed her new surroundings. The musty smell penetrated every inch of the room, and the dark walls pressed in on her from all sides. This wouldn't be easy to escape from, and she suspected that even if she managed to break out of the cell, plenty of guards would be waiting for her throughout the barracks, ready to take her back down again.

She sank onto the thin pallet lying in the corner of the room and took a deep breath, trying to calm herself so that she could think clearly enough to devise a plan. Across from her cell was an iron gate barred and secured with a lock larger than her hand. Who was she kidding? She was stuck here until someone let her out.

It was then that she thought of the dwarves. They would know she was gone by now, and it wouldn't take them long to discover where she had disappeared to. Would they attempt to rescue her? She certainly hoped not. They wouldn't stand a chance against these savage giants. But she knew they would try.

Her dwarves had the warrior spirits of their ancestors. She had become family to them. They wouldn't give her up without a fight. She wished she had never met them. A sad smile bloomed on her face. It was the first time in her life she ever remembered caring for someone else more than she cared for herself. What a strange feeling.

Queen Stelia personally led her troops through the forest for this mission. With her army so nearby, her spies had finally gained enough courage to venture into the woods surrounding the ogre kingdom. While they hadn't seen the princess, they had found the dwarves' cottage, where a single, long dress hung on the clothesline beside seven short shirts. Some girl lived with them, and out here, in the middle of nowhere, the chances that it was some other human girl were slim.

Her men surrounded the clearing, waiting, watching to see if anyone was inside. No one stirred, no smoke rose from the chimney, and no sounds came from within. The queen motioned to a few of her knights, and they cautiously slipped forward towards the small house. One tried the door and found it unlocked, so they slid inside.

Everything appeared perfectly ordinary; hot coals lay in the hearth, seven unmade beds stood to one side, several chairs sat around a clean table, and a long couch with a pillow and folded blanket set neatly on one end filled a nook on one side of the room.

The queen entered behind them and smirked when she saw that pillow and blanket. If Princess Nixa was the girl living here, Stelia found it amusing that she had sunk so low as to sleep on the couch of such a quaint little cottage. But she needed more proof. She didn't want to waste her time here if this was just some village girl.

The queen scanned the room, looking for anything she could identify as belonging to the princess, and suddenly, she noticed something—a cloak hanging off one of the chairs near the fireplace. She had seen Nixa wear it on many occasions at the castle. She'd finally found her.

Stelia couldn't wait until the girl returned to the cottage that night. With the house so close to the mountain, there must be a mine nearby. That's where they would be. A soldier met her as she exited the simple dwelling.

"There's a trail, Your Majesty, leading to the mountains."

"Let's go."

The soldier motioned for the others to follow, and the group headed toward the caves.

As they approached the trail's end, they could hear a commotion from the tunnels inside. The dwarves were calling out Nixa's name. And they were coming closer. The queen motioned the troops back to the tree line. They waited, swords drawn.

A young dwarf rushed out first, frantically looking around, calling for Nixa. The queen waited until all seven emerged before she gestured her soldiers forward. They surrounded the surprised men, immediately cutting off any attempts to fight by pressing their swords against their necks.

"So, you have her!" snarled Brulin. The dwarves frantically looked around as much as they could with the soldiers' swords so close.

"Where is she?" asked Garroth, his voice high with desperation.

The queen tapped her finger against her lips, studying the men. Their breathing came out rough, and their eyes stared wildly. Panic was etched on every line of their faces. They didn't know where the princess was either. Interesting. But they must have some idea, some guess.

"I don't have her," Stelia said, watching their reactions carefully.

They glanced at each other uneasily.

"But you already suspected that, didn't you?"

None of the men would meet her gaze.

"Of course not," said Brulin.

The queen slowly walked around the group, eyeing each of them carefully, looking for weaknesses. She came to a stop before Harnic. He looked everywhere but at her. She stood quietly, staring at him, her hands on her hips. Finally, he nervously glanced up. Her intense gaze held him.

"You know where she is."

"No," he whispered.

"Where is she?"

"I don't know." He shuffled his feet and looked away.

"Where is she?"

His eyes shot back up to her and then away again.

"I don't know where she is."

"Tell me where the princess is."

"I don't know." His voice came out as a whimper.

"Leave him alone," yelled Durfal.

"You *will* tell me where Nixa is. Either you will tell me now, and I'll let you and your brothers go, or you'll tell me later after my torturer has had his fun with you. Either way, you will tell me. Why not spare yourselves all the pain and give me the information now?"

"I don't know where she is." His voice squeaked in fear.

"Take them," the queen commanded her men. "And search the caves and the nearby forest. She's been with them recently, or they wouldn't have called out for her. She must be somewhere nearby.

The captain called out orders directing the soldiers to their tasks, and the queen followed the prisoners back to their camp. *Soon*, she told herself, *soon*.

# Chapter 5

Nixa had finally drifted off into a fitful sleep when her cell door slammed open. Without a word, a guard grabbed her from her mat, pulling her out the door and up the stairs. Three other guards met them on the main floor and followed them as they made their way down the passage toward the barracks door. Nixa scrambled after him as quickly as she could. After all this rough treatment, she would definitely have a bruise on that arm.

They made their way toward the castle's courtyard, and as they rounded the corner, the castle itself came into view. It took Nixa's breath away. The guards heard her gasp and actually stopped to let her admire it, their pride difficult to ignore.

The building stood over twice as large as her home, even larger than it would need to be to account for the difference in the sizes of humans and ogres. White stone decorated in gold leaf made up the outer wall. The gold reflected the light of the glowing orbs hanging overhead and illuminated the space as brightly as an above-ground day. The barracks had been situated in a shadowy corner. Her eyes couldn't adjust to the brightness before her fast enough, and she had to shade them from the glow.

Nixa followed the lines of the walls up and noticed ogre warriors stationed at various levels going almost to the top of towers that pointed like daggers at the cavern ceiling. They would be challenging to get past. She gazed up even further and saw faint beams of light shining down through crevices in the cavern roof. Holes in the cavern's ceiling presented some possibilities, especially since she saw several winding paths headed up along the cavern walls. When her guard noticed the direction of her eyes, he roughly pushed her forward again.

They made their way to the two iron doors that served as entrance to the castle. The guards raised their fists in salute as they approached, and the doors swung open. The guard pulling Nixa along slowed his pace, walking through the grand corridors, giving his prisoner time to take in the beauty of her surroundings.

She felt both admiration and horror at the intricate paintings and carvings that covered the walls. Scenes of ogres engaged in battle with dragons and giant pythons decorated the space. Bloody battles, full of flying body parts and gore. Some details were done in gold and silver and even covered with bright gemstones. It was both beautiful and horrible.

Thick tapestries also hung at intervals along the corridor. These portrayed scenes even more horrendous to Nixa, those of ogres ripping apart human bodies. She shuddered at the images and heard light chuckles from the ogre guards behind her.

Those laughs made something snap in Nixa. She had felt nothing but fear since she'd encountered the guards. Her terror had reached heights she had never known before. But no more. It was as if a switch had been flipped in her mind. All the fear and tension that had built up in her this whole time evolved into a blinding rage. She saw red.

Her whole demeanor changed. Where she had been walking slightly bent in on herself, her back suddenly straightened. Her head, which had previously been bowed low, shot up, and her eyes became steel, glaring straight ahead.

The guards noticed the change. The one gripping her arm snorted and pulled her along even faster. She hurried to keep up, but she kept her head high. The throne room doors were even more elegantly designed than any other surface she had seen so far, but she didn't spare them more than a glance. Guards opened the doors as they approached, and Nixa glided in as best as she could, given the situation.

She ignored the splendor of the room, the tall statues lining the walls, the vaulted ceiling, and the crystal chandeliers. She avoided looking at the shine of the marble floor. Instead, her gaze shot to the front of the room and landed immediately on the massive being seated on the throne. Her eyes widened in surprise. This was not what she had expected.

Other than the fact that he was half again as big as any human she knew and that his ears came to a sharp point, he looked like someone she would have admired in her father's court. If she forced herself to be honest, she would have to admit that he was much more handsome than any man she had ever met before, at court or elsewhere.

He let her stare, laughter dancing in his eyes at her bewilderment. When she noticed, this only served to rekindle her anger.

"I demand you release me at once!" she insisted.

The ogre king quirked a brow. "You demand? You are not in any position to make demands, little girl."

Nixa seethed at the patronizing address. True, they were all huge compared to her, compared to any human, but the term "little girl" just seemed so demeaning.

"I am NOT a 'little girl.' I am a princess, and I expect to be treated like one!"

The king snorted. "You sound more like an ogre with that attitude. I would expect a human princess to show more restraint and decorum."

She fumed. "Restraint! Decorum! You are holding me against my will. Such hostility could lead to war between our kingdoms."

The king laughed and slapped the arm of his throne. "Excellent! I haven't had a good war in ages. How does that sound, boys? Want to go to war?"

A roar of agreement filled the room, and Nixa glanced around at the hoard of warriors watching their exchange.

Shock flitted across her face. She hadn't expected that response, but contemplation quickly replaced the shock. This may be a good thing. If the ogres went to war with her kingdom and won, at least her stepmother would be off the throne. But it wouldn't help her unless she could get the ogres on her side, have them put her on the throne in her mother's place.

King Vrag laughed again as he noticed the myriad emotions dart across her face.

"Don't think to trick or manipulate me, little girl. I know what is happening in your kingdom, and I know where you stand." He leaned forward, resting his elbows on his knees. "I will not be using my army to help you regain your throne. If that is your plan, you must do it alone." He leaned back in his seat. "However, before you can do so, you will have to find a way to escape my domain."

The king waved his arm, taking in the vast city that could be seen through the tall windows of the throne room. "And you will not find that so easy to accomplish. No. I think I'll keep you for a while. You amuse me."

Nixa sputtered. "How dare you, sir! I am a princess, and I will not be treated like some common prisoner."

"You will be treated like an ogre prisoner and kept in the dungeon if you continue behaving in that manner. If you want to be treated like a guest and enjoy the luxury of a guest room, then I expect you to act like a visiting princess should act. Which would you prefer?"

Nixa bit the inside of her cheek. "I would like to stay in a guest room," she muttered.

The king looked at her expectantly.

"If it please Your Majesty," she added with a stiff curtsey, her tone flat and hard.

The ogre king nodded, a smirk on his face. "Very well. We shall prepare a room for you." He signaled to his guards. "Take her to the guest quarters and make sure she doesn't try anything foolish."

Once again, Nixa found herself being dragged down strange corridors. When she was shoved into a room and the door locked behind her, Nixa surveyed her surroundings emotionlessly. She felt numb from everything she had recently experienced. She knew she would have to try to come up with a plan of action soon, but she was drained. She had nothing left. Even the rage that had filled her just moments ago was gone. She walked to the bed, lay down, and closed her eyes.

A loud bang reverberated through the room, jerking Nixa awake. Startled, she jolted up in bed. The ogre king strolled into her bedroom, stopping by her bedside and staring down at her as if his actions were completely normal.

"What is the meaning of this?" she yelled, pulling the blanket up to her chin.

The king motioned a servant forward. Nixa leaned back as she approached. The ogre girl, hunched over, gave Nixa a pleading glance. Nixa watched her warily but didn't move again. The girl leaned toward her and fastened a gold collar around her neck.

"What is this supposed to be?" asked Nixa, waving her hand at the heavy ornament. The girl pulled a long gold-colored chain from a pouch on her waist while Nixa's eyes were fixed on the king. She didn't notice what the servant was doing until the chain was attached to the collar, and both had been secured in place with a small lock.

The princess reached up to feel the restraint, and her eyes widened in disbelief. She watched helplessly as the servant gave the other end of the chain to the king, and he attached it to a wide, metal band on his wrist.

"I've decided that you would make a good pet," he said, pulling on the chain until she fell forward across the bed.

Oh, how she hated this creature!

"I'm nobody's pet," she ground out through clenched teeth.

"Tsk, tsk, tsk," said the king condescendingly. "Are you being naughty?" The words sounded ridiculous in his deep, gravelly voice. "Naughty pets get punished." His eyes narrowed, and his lips spread into a sinister grin.

Fear and humiliation shot through Nixa, but it couldn't compete with the anger rising through her entire being.

"Do what you want," she said. "You're going to anyway. I'm not afraid of you."

"Very well." The smile fled from his face as he motioned a guard forward. The guard pulled a short whip off his belt as he approached. Nixa shut her eyes tightly and braced herself for the blow. But none came. Instead, she heard the whip strike flesh, followed by a low whimper.

Opening her eyes, she turned to the sound. The servant girl knelt on the floor sobbing quietly as the guard struck her again.

"Stop! You monster!" She jumped down from the bed and knelt beside the girl.

"Are you okay?"

The ogre girl just looked up briefly, then lowered her head into her hands.

"Fine! I'll be your pet. Just leave her alone." Nixa glared at the king. He laughed as he unclasped her chain from his wrist.

"Get her cleaned up and dressed. I want to see her in my office in an hour."

The servant girl nodded meekly. Nixa helped her up off the ground as the door slammed behind the king and his guard.

King Vrag held in his laugh until he reached the end of the corridor. He turned and slapped his hand on the shoulder of the guard with the whip.

"Excellent job. Both of you. Your daughter was so convincing she almost had me believing you'd hurt her."

"Benodin's having a blast, I'm sure. She's always been a good actress. She'll get your little human whipped into shape in no time."

With another laugh, the men continued down the hall.

Nixa sat the girl down on the bed and turned her so she could examine her back. As soon as she tried to undo her dress, the ogre flinched away from her.

"I need to check your wounds."

The girl shook her head. "I'll have mama see to them later." She jumped off the bed and hurried to a door on the side of the room.

"We need to get you in the bath, so you won't be late meeting the king."

Nixa started to argue, but she recognized the same flash of determination in the girl's eyes that she had often felt in her own.

"What's your name?" she asked.

"Benodin, Your Highness," the girl replied with a curtsey.

"Thank you for your help, Benodin. I would like a bath very much."

She followed the girl into the adjoining chamber and let out a sudden breath. The splendor that abounded in the rest of the castle also extended here. They had never had anything as grand in her home.

White marble covered the walls, and polished stone gleamed on the floor. A thoughtfully arranged selection of soaps, oils, and salts filled a tray next to the edge of the tub. The calming scent of lilies, roses, and citrus wafted into the air. Fluffy towels hung to one side, and piles of soft cloths were neatly folded on another shelf.

In the center of the room stood a colossal bathtub made of polished marble, large enough to fit four people comfortably or perhaps two ogres, which made more sense. After all, everything was larger here.

Benodin turned on the faucet. Nixa watched the steaming water fill the tub as Benodin helped her out of her dress. The annoying chain constantly got in the way, somewhat ruining Nixa's pleasure at the thought of a relaxing bath. But not completely.

Benodin gathered Nixa's dirty clothes and left the chamber, giving her some welcome privacy.

She stepped into the tub and sank into its inviting warmth. The heat soothed her tired muscles as she submerged herself fully. She had forgotten how wonderful a hot bath could feel. She'd only had the cold creek to bathe in at the dwarves' cottage, that and a basin of hot water for a sponge bath every morning. This felt heavenly in comparison.

When the water cooled, she finally emerged. Benodin appeared as if by magic and helped her dress in a new gown. The light blue material felt like clouds brushing against her skin, hugging her torso snuggly and billowing out elegantly below her waist. It fit her perfectly. Curious, Nixa twirled before the mirror.

"How did you find a dress that fits so well?" she asked Benodin. "And so quickly."

Benodin ushered her over to the dressing table and sat her in the chair.

"Magic."

Nixa waited for more, but the ogre girl silently began arranging her hair.

"Magic?"

Benodin met her eyes in the mirror.

"Okay, I probably shouldn't say anything, but some ogres have transformation magic. We can transform anything into anything else. We just got the measurements of your dress and transformed another one into the same size."

"Really? I mean, I'd heard that you had magic, but I didn't realize it would be so..."

"Useful?"

Nixa nodded.

"It can be at times."

Benodin pinned up her natural curls to fall in long, ebony waves down her back. "Your hair is so pretty. I've never seen hair so dark or skin so pale if it's not rude of me to say so."

Nixa laughed. "No, it's not rude. My mom used to call me Snow White when I was little, and that's what my full name means in the old language. She said my skin was as white as snow."

"So, all humans aren't like that."

"No, humans come in all shades, from the blackest black to the whitest white and all variations of brown in between."

"Hmph. You certainly are a colorful lot."

"Are ogres not the same?" asked Nixa, trying not to stare at the girl's skin. At first glance, it had appeared dusky, like the others, but upon closer inspection, she noticed a subtle undertone of blue.

"Not really. Some of us have more blue or gray in our skin than others, but the difference isn't noticeable unless you get close."

"Well, I think your skin is beautiful."

Benodin grinned. "Thanks. I think yours is, too." She put the last pin in and fluffed up the back of Nixa's hair. "How does that look?"

"Beautiful," Nixa said with a grin.

"Good, now you're ready to greet the king."

Nixa suddenly frowned, her good mood vanishing instantly.

"Don't be like that," said Benodin, noticing her change in demeanor. "He's really not that bad."

Nixa swiveled around to stare at the girl in astonishment. "How can you say that? He just had you beaten for something you didn't do."

Benodin glanced down at the carpet. "It didn't hurt that bad," she mumbled.

"I wish you'd let me look at it."

"No, no. It's fine. I had my mom tend to it while you were in the bath.

Benodin bent over and picked up the gold chain where it had been lying on the floor.

"You might want to wrap this around your wrist, so it doesn't get stuck on anything."

Nixa grabbed it and twisted the long chain around her arm.

"Yeah, he's not that bad," she said sarcastically.

Benodin stifled a laugh. "I know he seems that way, but he's just having a joke at your expense."

"Well, I don't think it's funny," Nixa huffed.

Benodin giggled. "I can tell. But look on the bright side. He wouldn't be doing this if he didn't like you."

"I shudder to think how he would treat me if he hated me."

# Chapter 6

Nixa sat on a low stool by the king's desk chair. Standing next to him was bad enough, but with her practically sitting on the ground beside him, she really did feel like a pet. The top of her head barely reached his armrests, the perfect height for him to reach over and pat her hair.

Which he did.

Quite often.

Nixa spent her days with an almost constant scowl on her face.

Benodin had stopped pinning her hair up days ago since the style never lasted more than a few minutes in the king's company. He seemed to get a strange pleasure from pulling the pins out and running his fingers through the long tresses while he conducted business. No one he met with paid her any more attention than a human would pay to a cat or dog sitting on the floor by their master.

Nixa had been following him around everywhere for a week now. The anger at her position she'd felt in the beginning was still there. It simmered inside her deep down, never entirely vanishing. But over the last few days, it had altered a bit. She still felt angry at her situation most of the time, but now her anger was also directed at herself almost as much as it was directed at the insufferable ogre.

Benodin was right, she had to admit. Other than the demeaning and completely unacceptable way he was treating her, he wasn't that bad. And he never hurt her. Neither had he hurt Benodin again, but then, she had made sure not to give him any reason to.

Truthfully, Nixa enjoyed sitting in on King Vrag's meetings. The interesting discussions often distracted her from her simmering rage. She was learning a lot, she told herself, when she felt guilty for being drawn into the conversations. When she escaped, this information could be useful.

They discussed troop movements, merchant routes, and supply chains, all as if the princess of a rival kingdom wasn't sitting at his feet listening to every word. He clearly considered her absolutely no threat at all.

Theoretically, that could work in her favor. It never hurt to be underestimated. The problem was he wasn't underestimating her. She was no threat. He had her so secure she had no hope of escape. Guards constantly stood watch outside her chamber when she was there, and she was always chained to the king when she was not.

Nixa shifted on her stool, and King Vrag absentmindedly began patting her head. She hated the pats. Nixa wouldn't admit it, even to herself, but if she *were* honest, she didn't hate the feel of him running his hands through her hair. That was quite soothing. That is, if she didn't think about the insulting game he was playing. But she hated the pats.

As the days passed, and she grew more familiar with the workings of the ogre court and more interested in the issues they faced, it gradually became more challenging to remember to focus on the insult of her position and to hold onto her anger. The ogre kingdom flourished under King Vrag. He punished criminals harshly and protected his citizens fiercely. He was a fair and just ruler. Nixa often sat with him when he held court and listened as he brought judgment to the cases that came before him. He rarely made any decision that Nixa disagreed with, and when he did, the difference could easily be explained as cultural rather than ethical.

She felt like she was beginning to see who he was as a person. But once the meetings were over, and he pulled her after him like a reluctant kitten, her anger would always resurface. While she was learning more about him, he didn't seem to care to discover anything about her. He never asked her any questions or even talked to her, except to say, "Good little human; bad little human; eat your food, little human," and other such patronizing things.

Until one day, all of that suddenly changed. Nixa awoke that morning to the sight of him standing over her, staring down at her with his arms crossed tightly and a fierce glare marring the lines of his handsome face. She just stared back at him, not sure what she had done to warrant such a look.

"What?" she finally asked.

"You need to learn self-defense."

"Why?"

He snorted but continued staring. "I have no idea. You are quite lovely, I suppose, in a small, weak, human sort of way. But you're so small and weak. And human.

I can't imagine why he would be interested in you that way. But apparently, he is, so you need to learn to defend yourself." He turned to Benodin.

"Get her dressed. I'll wait in the hall."

Benodin rushed over and practically pulled Nixa out of bed.

"What's going on?" she asked as her lady's maid jerked her nightgown over her head and stuffed her arms into a dress.

"There're rumors going around that Duke Burig asked if he could buy you from the king. He claimed that he could think of many ways to entertain himself with such a beautiful female pet."

Nixa paled. "You don't think he wants to..."

"That's exactly what he wants."

Benodin pulled a brush through Nixa's long tresses.

"The king doesn't think of you that way, apparently, but he knows how stubborn and determined Duke Burig can be when he gets something in his mind. You're safe as long as you're here under King Vrag's protection, but he can't keep you by his side constantly. If nothing else, you come back here every night to sleep. Duke Burig has a great deal of influence. There's no telling what he would do to get his hands on you now that he's decided he wants you. King Vrag only wants you to be able to fight back in case you find yourself in a situation where you need to. There, you're done." Benodin pushed Nixa toward the chamber door. "Don't keep the king waiting."

Nixa stared at the array of weapons lining the walls of the training room: huge swords, axes, maces, and spears that must weigh so much that no human man could wield them long in battle. Many would not even be able to lift them.

Vrag stood beside her in front of a large table, littered with daggers of all sizes.

"You're too small and weak to wield an axe or spear, but you have long arms and legs and can move quickly. I think daggers would be best for you. You can wield them in close combat, and they won't tire you out so quickly."

His hand hovered over a few of the weapons before stopping at the smallest one. Even still, it was larger and heavier than the one she had strapped in her boot, but she wasn't about to inform him of that one.

He held it out to her, handle first, and she closed her hand around it, testing its weight. Captain Uenk stepped up to them and bowed before the king. "Your Majesty," he said gravely. "With your permission, I would like to train the young lady in hand-to-hand combat as well as in the use of daggers."

"Hmm, do you think she could get anywhere with hand-to-hand combat? She's so small."

Nixa pressed her lips together tightly. She was really getting tired of that man calling her small and weak. One of these days, she'd show him small and weak. She stood there fuming while he calmly discussed the best training regime for her with the captain. Suddenly, she realized that his heart was right in front of her face. Well, at least not *too* far above her eye level. She was sure she could reach it easily enough if she tried. And she *did* have a dagger in her hand.

Common sense fled. She didn't think about how the captain would see what she did. She didn't think about how she couldn't possibly escape. All she could think of was the collar around her neck trapping her here, his heart beating a few inches away, and the dangerous bit of steel she gripped tightly in her hand. Without further thought, almost as if it were a reflex, she raised the dagger and stabbed it toward his heart.

So fast she didn't see him move, his hand shot up and grabbed her wrist, twisting it until she dropped the weapon. It fell to the ground with a loud clink.

The infuriating man hadn't even paused in his conversation. He continued talking as though nothing had happened. However, he didn't release her wrist. She pulled back against his hold, using all the strength her fury gave her. She clawed at his fingers with her other hand and pulled back her leg and kicked him. That got their attention. The men turned their gazes down to her, only for the king to say, "You see, she has no skills whatsoever. A child could kill her without even trying."

The captain nodded. "I see what you mean. We won't be able to do much with her, but I can, at least, teach her some basic maneuvers."

"Do what you can." Vrag released her arm. Unbalanced by her struggles, she fell against him. She jerked away instantly and glared up into his laughing eyes. He turned and left her with the captain. Nixa stood there rubbing her aching wrist as she watched the king leave the room.

"Pick up your dagger," said the guard captain, watching her curiously. "If you want to have any chance of killing your master, you're going to have to learn how to fight properly."

Nixa turned to Uenk. The wicked grin that appeared on her face was in sharp contrast to the amused one on his.

Nixa followed Vrag down the hallway to her bedchamber after a long day of meetings, training sessions, and then more meetings. They'd just finished their evening meal, and Nixa looked forward to falling into her bed. Usually, when the ogre king dropped her off at the end of the day, he opened the door, unlatched her chain, and left. Benodin always waited for her inside.

Tonight, however, Benodin wasn't waiting inside, and Vrag followed her into the room, closing the door behind them. Nixa frantically searched for her maid, but she was nowhere to be found. She slowly turned to face the king. He stood there studying her intently, almost absentmindedly unhooking her chain.

"How is your training going?"

"I'm sure Captain Uenk has kept you updated."

"He has, but I want to hear what you think."

Nixa looked at him curiously. "Why?"

Vrag raised his brows. "Why not?

"You've never cared to know what I think about anything else. I am, after all, just your pet. Why would my opinion on anything matter?"

Vrag crossed his arms and leaned against the wall, blocking the door.

"Well, I care now. How do you think your training is going?"

Nixa sighed. She couldn't keep up with him. Was he trying to make her believe that he wanted her opinion?

"You know as well as I do that it's hopeless. I couldn't possibly take on one of you monsters in a fight."

Vrag growled. He pushed himself off the wall and stalked toward her menacingly. Nixa instinctively backed up at his approach until he had her hemmed in against the wall, his hands on the hard stone on either side of her head.

Nixa lost the ability to breathe. Heat flooded her body, and her mind stopped working.

"Fight me off," he said.

"What?"

"Fight me off. Show me what you've learned."

Nixa raised her hands and pressed against his chest, but of course, she couldn't budge him.

"Get away from me, you brute."

Vrag snarled at her. "Not good enough. Come on, little human, you can do better than that."

Nixa kicked his calf. She gasped as pain shot through her foot.

"Still not good enough. You better stop me," he said with a chuckle as he leaned closer.

Panic filled Nixa. She pushed harder against his chest. Was he going to kiss her? She couldn't let him kiss her. She didn't know why she felt this so strongly, but she did. She couldn't let him kiss her. She just couldn't.

She reached up and grabbed his neck, squeezing with both hands as hard as she could. He just moved one hand down and enclosed both of her wrists in it. Easily pulling them away and pressing them back up against the wall over her head. "Is that the best you've got? I will have to fire Uenk if he hasn't taught you anything better than this."

Nixa tried to think. She tried to remember what Captain Uenk told her to do in close encounters like this, but she couldn't remember anything. It was as if her mind had shut down completely. She was totally overwhelmed by his presence. All she could see was him. His earthy musk was the only thing she could smell. It permeated her senses. The sound of her heartbeat quickening filled her ears, and heat rushed through her body.

His face hovered only inches from hers, and the teasing expression it had held changed into something else. His gaze intensified and grew darker as his eyes locked onto hers. She didn't move. He slowly closed the distance and pressed his lips against hers. Sensations flooded her. She drowned in them as his lips moved sensually, sending her sinking farther into a mindless abyss.

All of a sudden, his grip on her wrists tightened, and he pulled away from her. Shock covered his face. He released her abruptly and stepped back. Nixa watched him warily. Her lips still tingled from the contact. She unconsciously pulled her bottom lip between her teeth. His eyes shot to the movement, and a growl escaped his throat. Turning quickly, Vrag stormed to the door, jerked it open, and disappeared down the hall.

A subdued Benodin entered behind him, glancing after the ogre as he made his hasty retreat. Nixa barely noticed her as the girl hurried over to check on her. When she didn't respond any more than to assure her she was okay, Benodin quietly helped her get ready for bed.

All Nixa could think of was that she shouldn't have let him kiss her. She couldn't physically stop him, but she felt confident that he would have stopped if she'd sincerely asked him to. Why had she let him? Why had she liked it? He was the enemy. He was her captor. He treated her like a pet! She hated him! But that had felt so good. Ugh!

She didn't even notice when Benodin blew out the candle and left. She lay there in the darkness, her mind in tumult. She had to get out of there. She couldn't stay here with him any longer. Nixa sobbed into her pillow. She had to escape, but part of her didn't want to leave. Part of her wanted to stay with him, and she felt disgusted at herself for that. What was wrong with her? Nixa finally cried herself to sleep in the early hours of the morning.

# Chapter 7

S hortly before dawn, Nixa woke to find another ogre sitting on the couch across from her bed. *Why?* she thought. Why could she not be rid of these creatures? She groaned and turned her back to him, burying her face in her pillow. When he noticed she had woken, the man rose and ambled over to her.

"He's never going to let you go, you know. It doesn't matter if you're here as a spy or hiding from the queen. You belong to him now. You're his pet, and he never lets go of what is his."

The ogre waved his arm around the room. "This is your life now...unless."

"Unless?" she mumbled into her pillow.

The man shrugged. "Unless the king dies."

"And is the king going to die?"

"He could if you're not afraid of getting your hands dirty and taking a little risk. I heard about what you did in the training room. It was sloppy and not well thought out, but it shows that you have potential."

Not only had she not planned that attack in advance, but she wasn't even thinking when she'd tried to execute it. Lying here with a clear head contemplating murder was an entirely different matter. She had hired an assassin before and had tried to again, but she'd never actually killed someone with her own hands. The thought of it felt different somehow, especially after what had just happened.

"Why are you talking to me about this?" she asked, turning to face him. "After all, I'm only a weak little human. You heard how the incident in the training room turned out."

The man crossed his arms, and his gaze traveled over her body.

"Yes, you are. And you're a pretty one at that. But that is exactly why you are the one to do it. You aren't a threat. He lowers his guard around you because you are so harmless. You're the only one who can get close enough."

"Who are you?" she asked him, sitting up in the bed.

"Duke Burig, at your service."

Nixa groaned.

"I see you've heard of me."

"Look, even if what you say is true, it still wouldn't work," said Nixa, ignoring the comment. "Vrag's guards are around him all the time. He might lower his guard around me, but I doubt they do."

The duke quirked a brow, and the left side of his lip raised in a half smile.

"Fine, they probably do too, but no matter how much he lowers his guard, he moves too quickly. My actions in the training room didn't even interrupt his conversation. He didn't even look down at me when he stopped me." She raised her hands helplessly. "How can I possibly defeat that?"

Burig rubbed his chin thoughtfully. "You're right. You'll have to catch him completely unawares. I've got it! You can kill him in his sleep. He'll be alone and completely helpless then."

Nixa turned her head and glanced at the man askance. "Why would I be around him while he slept?" Had word of what happened last night spread already? Were people assuming things about her?

"Don't worry. I think I can arrange that."

"No. I don't want you to arrange that. I have no desire to be alone with that man in his rooms at night," said Nixa sternly.

"Do you want to escape from here? Do you ever want to see the light of day again?"

Of course, she did. But what would it cost her?

"What exactly do you have in mind?"

"I have made the king aware of my interest in you, and he is not pleased."

"Neither am I."

Burig ignored the interruption. "He knows that you are most vulnerable in your chambers at night. Now that I've managed to get in here, he'll be furious. I'll have to lie low for a while, but he'll also be more cautious. I have no doubt he'll move you into his rooms, where he can keep an eye on you at all times."

"What! No! I don't want that."

"Too bad," the duke replied with an evil grin. "I'm already here." He glanced out the window at the rising sun. "Your maid should be arriving soon. All I need to do is wait for her. She'll set up such a cry that the guards will come running. There's no way to stop what has been set in motion."

Things went just as he had predicted. When Benodin saw him standing by the bed, she sent the maid following her with the water pitcher back into the hall for the guards. Duke Burig bowed politely to them both.

"Enjoy your new quarters. I'll be in touch," he said before casually walking out the door. He managed to get away before the guards returned to their posts. Word of his intrusion spread quickly. Captain Uenk arrived with new guards, and the old ones, who had been bribed away from the princess's rooms, were taken for questioning. Almost immediately after, a retinue of servants came and began packing Nixa's belongings. She groaned and fell back onto her bed.

Nixa didn't see Vrag that entire day, but she was never alone. Benodin stuck to her like the maid had been chained to *her* wrist. Four guards followed her around as well, even going so far as to enter the ogre king's chambers with her and stand guard inside as she settled in. A small bed had been set up for her in a side room, but he'd had the door removed from its hinges.

Nixa sat in a chair by the fireplace, her feet pulled up on the seat and her arms wrapped around her legs. The stream of servants bringing in and unpacking her new clothes had left a long time ago. Now, she glanced at the bed, clearly visible through the open doorway. At least she was given that much consideration. She'd half expected to sleep on a pillow on the floor like a real pet. She shuddered in horror. Or he could have wanted her to sleep at the foot of his bed like a dog. It could have been much worse, but still, she wished she had a door.

The light in the room dimmed as the evening waned. Benodin brought her something to eat, and she nibbled on it distractedly. All day, her brain had worked frantically. She had to get out of there, no matter how she might want to stay.

Because she wanted to stay.

Duke Burig's arguments sounded convincing. King Vrag probably wouldn't let her go, not if his response to this incident was any indication. She could never escape chained to his wrist every day and sleeping in his rooms every night. Her only chance for freedom lay with the ogre king's death. Even then, could she escape? Did guards stand outside his chamber at night? It seemed unlikely that he would want that. After all, he was the fierce and powerful ogre king. How would it look if he had to have others protect him? But then again, he was the king. The position would call for extra security.

Nixa chewed her lip in thought. She would have to take the risk; otherwise, she'd never leave this place. A greater concern lurked at the back of her mind. She couldn't forget that kiss. And now she was staying in his chambers. What had that expression of shock and horror on his face after he kissed her meant? Was he disgusted at what he had done? If not, what?

She watched the flames dance and considered. She would have to try to kill him again, but this time, she would plan things out—no more acting on impulse. Various scenarios ran through her head. Duke Burig was right about one thing: her only chance of success would be to get him while he slept.

Captain Uenk had taught her quick ways to take someone out. Of those, she figured her best bet would be to cut his throat. She shivered at what she was considering doing. Could she do it? She had to. It was the only way. She'd wait an hour or so after he'd fallen asleep before she attempted it.

Her plan made, such as it was, she rose from the chair and headed into her bedroom. She should get changed before he returned since he wasn't going to allow her any privacy. Benodin jumped up from the window seat, where she had been quietly resting, and followed the princess to help her get ready for the night.

Nixa had been in bed fighting sleep for about half an hour before Vrag returned. She heard him dismiss Benodin and walk to the doorway of her room, but she pretended to sleep, so he finally left. She listened as he undressed and settled in. Then came the hard part. She waited.

A couple of times, she caught herself drifting off and pricked her finger on her dagger to keep herself awake. She tried to force her eyes open as much as possible so they would adjust to the darkness, but she didn't dare sit up, not before she was sure he slept soundly enough that the motion wouldn't disturb him. After she thought it had been long enough, she slowly slid out of her bed.

Hardly daring to breathe, she quietly made her way into his room and crept up to his still form. Soft light from the fireplace illuminated the sleeping man, and she almost gave up then. He looked so peaceful in his sleep. So unthreatening. Not harmless by any means. His muscles bulged in the arms he had resting over his head on the pillow, and his bare chest, revealed above the blanket, could have been carved from stone. No, he didn't look harmless. But the strong line of his jaw and his high cheekbones didn't seem quite as harsh in this relaxed posture. And his long white hair fanned out around his head like a halo.

*I can't do this*, thought Nixa turning away. She stared out the window at the sphere-lit courtyard, tears sliding down her cheeks. Memories of her brief time with the dwarves flashed through her mind. She'd been happy there. It was the first place she'd ever lived that she had felt loved. They had become family to her. If she didn't find a way to escape, they would eventually come looking for her, and they would die. She had to do this for them as much as for herself.

Nixa turned back to the bed. Vrag seemed to be sleeping peacefully, his thick chest rising and falling with steady breaths. She carefully raised the dagger and held it just above his throat. She couldn't seem to make her hand move any closer. She stood there like that for a few seconds before she stepped back with a silent sob and dropped the knife on the rug.

As soon as she moved, Vrag sat up in bed, grabbed her around the waist and pulled her onto the mattress with him. Nixa gasped as he held her wrists imprisoned on each side of her head.

"You'll regret that, little human," he said with a snarl.

"But I didn't do it," she replied, whimpering. "I couldn't do it."

"And that is what you'll regret."

"You wanted me to kill you?"

He barked out a laugh. "I'm not so easy to kill as that, little one."

"You knew," she said accusingly. She struggled against his hold. "The whole time. You knew."

"Of course, I knew." He adjusted his position over her, instantly stopping her struggles. "You do not make a good assassin, my pet."

"Please let me go," she whispered. His gaze softened, and he leaned off her, pulling her up with him.

"Do you really hate me so much?" he asked, sitting up on the bed beside her.

Nixa hesitantly looked him in the eyes. "I don't hate you. I do, but I don't. I don't know what I feel. I just don't like being trapped here."

"Is it because you're my prisoner or because you're my pet?" He reached out and picked up a strand of her hair, watching it fall through his fingers.

"I don't mind being by your side, but it hurts when you treat me in such a demeaning way. I don't want to sit at your feet and be ignored all day. I don't want to be a possession."

"What do you want?" He leaned in close, and her breath hitched. He continued playing with her hair.

What did she want? It was becoming more difficult to think, but she had to stay focused.

"I want," she started, "my freedom."

"No."

"Then, if I'm going to have to remain your prisoner, I want to be allowed to stay in my room all day and not be paraded around as your pet."

"No. I'm not going to let you out of my sight anymore. Try again."

"Then, I want this collar gone. I want to walk and sit by your side as a person. I want you to talk to me. I want you to stop patting me on the head like a little puppy dog."

Vrag's fingers stilled in her hair. Nixa blushed as she finally admitted, "I don't mind this. I just don't like the head pats."

Vrag smiled and continued playing with her dark strands. "Good, because I love the way your hair feels against my skin. Anything else?"

Nixa considered. "I want a curtain hung in my doorway so I can have a little privacy."

Vrag clearly didn't like that. Nixa held her breath while he thought it over. "Okay, but I can enter whenever I wish to make sure you're safe."

"Alright, but you have to give me some warning first in case I'm not dressed."

Clearly reluctant, Vrag nodded. "Is that all, my demanding pet?"

Nixa considered telling him to stop calling her "pet" and "little human," but she had grown accustomed to it. She didn't want to push him too far, so she let it go.

She shook her head. Then she grabbed her hair out of his hands and swept it all behind her. Sticking out her neck with her head bent to the side, she waited.

Vrag's breath caught at her vulnerable pose. To expose her neck like that to an enemy... Obviously, she didn't fear him as much as she should. Though, he had less desire at the moment to injure that neck than he had to kiss it.

Forcing out a lighthearted chuckle, he rose from the bed and walked over to his desk. Opening the top drawer, he pulled out a small key. He sat back down beside her and gave her a hard stare. "You must promise me you won't try to escape."

"That wasn't part of the deal." Her voice sounded stronger as her confidence began to return.

"Fine," he snapped as he unlocked her collar and removed the offending article. "Stopping you could be fun."

Once freed, Nixa moved around him and slid off the bed. "Then we can start our new arrangement tomorrow?"

"Tomorrow."

"Goodnight, King Vrag."

"Goodnight, Princess Nixa."

Garroth and Harnic sat huddled together in the corner of the cell. For the past several days, the guards had been coming and dragging them away, one by one. Most of them had already had their turn with the torturer and been left back in the cell battered and bloody.

The door opened again, and more guards barged in. They threw Durfal into the cell, face down and bruised. His eyes were closed as if he had been unconscious for some time.

Brulin, Ubril, Varfid, and Thondrak left their posts by the wall and went to check on him. Anger surged through them, a rage that started deep inside and welled up to spread throughout their bodies. Brulin felt it especially. Being the oldest, he had always looked out for the others. Now, all he could do was stand by and watch helplessly as that evil woman had his brothers beaten for information they wouldn't give. Princess Nixa was one of them. Every last dwarf in that cell would give his life for her just as they would for each other. Still, it wasn't easy watching them suffer.

The door slammed open again as more guards entered. They jerked Brulin out of the cell, threatening that Harnic would be next if he didn't tell them what they wanted to know. Brulin took a deep breath as they pulled him down the corridor. Harnic was the weakest and gentlest of them all. He would suffer the most from the torture. Perhaps… After all, if the princess was with the ogres as they suspected, it wasn't like the queen could get to her. She probably already guessed that was where she hid anyway. Could there be any harm in telling just that much? Maybe not, but he would stay silent, nonetheless. Gritting his teeth, Brulin braced himself for the pain.

What felt like hours later, the guards dragged Brulin, injured and miserable, back to the cell and threw him on the ground beside Harnic. As they reached for the younger dwarf, Brulin grabbed his arm.

"It's okay to tell them about the hole in the cave and where it led. You can say that she was curious about it, too, and that we think that's where she went," he whispered to his brother.

Harnic looked at him, eyes wide.

"It's okay?"

Brulin nodded. "I'm sure they've already found it anyway. Besides, they aren't going to be able to get her away from the ogres," he added with a forced chuckle.

The guards let him speak. When Brulin released his arm, they sneered at them and pulled Harnic to his feet and out the door. Brulin felt no remorse at his words. There was nothing that he said that could harm the princess, and divulging the information might save Harnic from unbearable pain. It would be alright.

# Chapter 8

Nixa awoke the next morning feeling better than she had felt in a long time. She stretched her arms over her head and let them rest against her pillow. She blushed as the action reminded her of the previous night. Heat flooded her body as she remembered how it had felt, his strong arms holding her in place, his body pressed against hers. With a quick shake of her head, Nixa shoved those thoughts out of her mind and jumped out of bed.

Benodin entered, carrying the breakfast tray followed by the other servant with the water pitcher. The lady's maid hummed in her deep ogre voice as she flittered around, setting the food on the little table. The other maid giggled before taking the empty tray and leaving the room.

Her joy must have been contagious because happiness flooded Nixa as well. At that moment, life seemed good. She was still a prisoner of that stubborn ogre, but that didn't bother her as much as it had. Things would change now. And maybe, in time, she could convince him to free her completely.

Nixa laughed when her large maid spun in a pirouette before bouncing over to help her out of her nightgown.

"What has you in such a good mood this morning?"

Benodin pointed to her unfettered neck. "I told you he was a good man. He's let you go."

Nixa rubbed her hand against the bare flesh. Yes, maybe he was. Maybe. She frowned, and the humming stopped.

"What's wrong?"

"Many people would say that my stepmother is a good woman. It's true; the kingdom does prosper under her rule, but it's not because she's a good woman. It's because she's a good businesswoman. She understands how to make a business, or in this case, a kingdom, succeed. She treats the people well only to gain their loyalty and best work. She knows that if they aren't happy, they won't work as hard. They'll rebel, and that will cost her money. She's very shrewd, my stepmother."

"King Vrag isn't that way," insisted Benodin, pulling the gown over her head a little harder than necessary.

"How can you say that?" asked Nixa, turning to the girl. She stood on her tiptoes to take the ogre's shoulders in her hands and look her square in the eyes. "He had you beaten for something you didn't do."

Benodin squirmed in her hold, so she released her.

"It didn't hurt," she mumbled.

"It sure looked like it did. But that's beside the point. He had you beaten!" Nixa watched her as she wandered over to the dressing table and started fidgeting with the perfume bottles.

"Promise you won't get mad."

"Why?" asked Nixa, her eyes narrowing and head tilting suspiciously.

"Well." Benodin wouldn't meet her gaze. She started playing with the bristles on the brush. "He didn't really have me beaten."

Confused, Nixa stared at the girl. "What do you mean? I was there. I saw it."

"Actually, that guard was my dad."

Comprehension slowly began to dawn. Nixa put her hands on her hips and glared at the girl. "The one who beat you?"

Benodin nodded, still refusing to look at the princess.

"It was all an act to get you to obey the king."

"Arg! I'll kill that man!" Nixa threw her arms up in exasperation, turned, and stalked over to the window, staring out into the courtyard below.

Benodin hurried over to her and tentatively touched her arm. "Please don't be angry with him. He does have a strange sense of humor, but you have to understand..."

Nixa looked up at the girl. "Understand what?"

"It's just that, well, I mean, no offense, but humans are not really considered ogres."

Nixa looked at her in confusion. "Of course, humans aren't considered ogres."

"No, I mean, they're not considered equal. We have always thought of them as less than." Benodin shrugged apologetically.

Nixa glared at her and turned back to the window.

"You have to admit," continued the girl in a rush, "you are all so tiny and fragile."

Nixa's back stiffened, but Benodin continued, trying to make the princess understand.

"And you aren't immortal. On your own. You live such short lives."

Nixa didn't move.

"It's just... Don't you understand? Ever since the end of the ogre-human wars, humans have been looked at as pets to us. Small, weak beings to take care of for their short lives. Fun little companions to dress up and show off to friends. It's very rare that they are anything else."

Nixa turned, and Benodin cringed when she saw the tear running down the princess's cheek.

"Rare, but not unheard of?"

Surprised, Benodin answered quickly. "No, not unheard of. There have been a few stories about ogres becoming true friends with humans, even fighting beside them in battle."

"That's all?" Nixa didn't know why she was disappointed, but she was.

"No," Benodin dragged out the word cautiously. "There have been a handful of incidents where ogres have married humans."

"And how did that go, with humans not being immortal?"

Benodin turned away from her and headed into the closet. She began rummaging through the gowns. "Don't worry about all that, Your Highness. It has nothing to do with you. Today is a beautiful day, and it's your first day free from your collar." She popped her head out of the room and held up a stunning red dress for Nixa's approval. "What do you think about this one? It will certainly get everyone's attention. And you always look so beautiful in red. It sets off your dark hair and red lips."

"Benodin."

"What?"

"What are you hiding from me?"

"Don't be ridiculous. Come, arms up." She raised the dress to pull it over Nixa's head, but the princess refused to move. She simply stood there staring at the girl.

"Fine," Benodin said with a huff. "But don't tell anyone I told you. I'd get in big trouble."

"Okay." Nix sat on the bed and patted the spot next to her. Benodin hung the gown back on the rack and sat down beside her.

"There is a way for a human to become immortal."

Nixa's brows shot up in surprise. "Really?"

Benodin nodded. "But it only happens when they bond with an immortal, and it doesn't always work."

"What happens if it doesn't work?"

"The human is either grossly disfigured, or they die. That's why it's frowned upon."

"Frowned upon?"

"It's never been declared illegal because rulers have always wanted to give the people the freedom to choose, but rarely does anyone attempt it."

"That's horrible. Why *would* anyone attempt it? The poor humans."

Benodin frowned at her. "They don't do it against their wills. It actually won't work at all unless both people care deeply for each other. Everyone knows that."

"Then why do they ever try it?"

"Love."

"I don't understand. That doesn't sound very loving to me."

Benodin grabbed one of the pillows, fluffed it up, and hugged it on her lap.

"It's the only way two people can be together forever if one is an ogre and the other a human. If they love each other, sometimes, they are willing to take the chance."

"I don't know," said Nixa. "It seems kind of selfish on the ogre's part to me. The human is, after all, the one who suffers if it fails."

Benodin bristled a little. "Are they? Think about it. If it doesn't work, the human will die, either immediately or slowly, from their deformities. The ogre will have to live his long life with the guilt of what he's done. If they genuinely love each other, can you imagine how horrible such a life would be? Ogres have long memories. The pain of that wouldn't fade quickly. He'd carry that burden with him for centuries if not millennia, and all because some human wanted to become immortal.

Nixa reached out and patted her arm. "I'm sorry. You're right. So." She started picking at the embroidered design on the bedcover. "How often does it work? I mean, what are the percentages?"

Benodin glanced at her sideways. "You're not thinking about trying to become immortal, are you?"

"No, no," She insisted. "I'm just curious."

Benodin eyed her suspiciously. "I don't know for sure. It's so rare that it's even attempted, and I'm sure we don't always know about it when it fails. Something like that is usually best kept secret."

"How many do you know of that have succeeded or failed?" Nixa wasn't sure why this was so important to her, but she felt like she had to know.

Benodin shrugged. "There was Yurot and Elania. Theirs worked. I think they're still living together on Algron Island. Valuk and Bethany's worked. They live in the swamps near Granville. Then, there was Xazig and Lenora. They live in the nether fields."

"But none here?"

"No. They usually leave the large cities since other people don't always understand. Here, we only have one big city in the mountain. They would probably leave the mountain to get away."

Nixa stared at her hands, her mind racing. "What about the ones that didn't succeed?"

Benodin sighed. "I've heard of five. Three of them ended up disfigured and died within a year. The other two died instantly."

"Why do they get disfigured? What exactly happens in the process?"

Benodin tossed her pillow on the bed. "Why are you so interested in this?"

"I don't know," admitted Nixa. She pulled her legs up on the bed and wrapped her arms around them. "I'm just curious."

Benodin huffed. "It is done in a bonding ceremony. What you would call a wedding." She picked the pillow back up and began pulling at the fringes.

"It sounds like the human is usually female."

Benodin laughed. "Of course. To ogre men, all females are smaller and weaker than they are, even ogre females, so falling in love with a human isn't too much of a stretch. But could you imagine an ogre female falling in love with a small, weak human? They're so skinny and frail." She snorted in disdain. "We like our men big and strong." She lifted her arms and flexed her muscles.

"Okay, okay," said Nixa, laughing at her maid's antics. "So, how does it work?"

Benodin put down her pillow and settled back against the bed. "Well, first they have the regular bonding, or marriage, ceremony, swearing an oath of loyalty and faithfulness, all that. Then, they exchange a blood bond, which involves them both drinking a potion made from a mixture of their blood that has been enchanted with powerful magic. This is also done as part of a normal bonding ceremony. This binds their essence together and makes it possible for them to share their life forces. Once the potion takes effect and the ogre's life force begins blending with the human's, the human becomes immortal."

She looked thoughtful for a moment before continuing. "The danger lies with the sharing of the life force. If one of them is human, having an ogre's life force invade her body... Well, I've heard that if the human doesn't have a strong enough life force of her own, the ogre's power can overwhelm her. It takes over and begins to transform her physically.

They never fully become ogres. Their human essence would have to be entirely eradicated for that to happen, but perhaps it would be better if they did. The partial transformation leaves them looking like dreadful monsters, with some appendages twice as large as others, facial features warped, spines twisted. The worst part is what happens internally. Some organs can grow abnormally large, crowding out others. Cancers can form throughout their bodies. It's all rather gruesome."

"Well, that doesn't sound pleasant," said Nixa, attempting to release some of the tension in the room.

Benodin snorted. "No, it doesn't, so don't get any ideas in that little human head of yours." She bonked Nixa on the nose, jumped up from the bed, and grabbed the abandoned dress.

Nixa was surprisingly unoffended at this unmaid-like behavior. She followed the girl and obediently lifted her arms for her dress.

"Now, let's get you beautified for our ogre king."

"He's not my king," muttered Nixa.

Benodin ignored her. She slipped the gown over her head and buttoned it up the back. She ran a brush quickly through her hair and pronounced her ready.

Nixa filed away the information she had learned that morning as she followed her guards down the hall toward the king's office. She told herself that she had only been curious, nothing more. After all, she had a strong curiosity. That's what had gotten her into this mess in the first place. From there, visions of the dwarves sprang to mind, and she wondered what they were doing. Maybe she would talk to Vrag about them. Perhaps he would let her get a message to them, letting them know she was safe.

Nixa heard raised voices as she approached the office door. The guards posted outside the entrance didn't seem concerned, though. They simply opened the door for her and stood aside, allowing her to enter. The first thing she noticed was the two large ogres standing threateningly close to each other, yelling. The second thing she noticed was the new chair sitting behind the desk next to an amused-looking ogre king. Ignoring the screaming men, Nixa waltzed past them and eased herself down into her new chair. Her happiness showed in her eyes, and Vrag smiled down at her, clearly pleased. Nixa blushed and turned her attention to the two men still arguing loudly.

"So let me make sure I understand," King Vrag held them both with an intense gaze, his booming voice filling the room, drowning out theirs. They both immediately fell silent.

"Boreg, you want to move the southern trade route to pass through the Kingdom of Mathyr and catch a ship at the elves' port, and you, Morek, want it to continue going through Ravendall, catching a ship at the human port. Since this involves a human kingdom, I'll let my pet decide." Vrag glanced down into Nixa's surprised eyes.

A smile played across his face as he watched the emotions cross hers.

Was he really going to let her make this decision? If so, she wouldn't disappoint him. Nixa looked at the two ogres staring at her in shocked silence. These men had been presenting their arguments to the king for days, and she had sat in on all those meetings. She had followed the discussions carefully and had already come to a conclusion. Nixa took a deep breath and began presenting her decision and the reasoning behind it.

The day was filled with one meeting after another, and the king often asked Nixa's opinion, usually to the chagrin of the other attendees. Logic dictated that she be exhausted after such a stream of intense discussions, but she wasn't. She had loved every minute of it. She'd been forced to listen in on these meetings for so long without being allowed to say anything. Several times, she'd felt like she would burst. Now that she could contribute, she was ecstatic.

Yet, she couldn't deny that it was nice to be with Vrag back in the privacy of their rooms. The constant shocked stares and angry scowls of the other ogres had been a little wearying. Benodin kept shooting Nixa telling glances as she sat their food out on the table. She didn't say anything even though Vrag was in the bathroom. Ogre's have excellent hearing. But Nixa knew what she was thinking as if she had spoken out loud. *See, he isn't so bad.* She would have heard about her contributions during the meetings by now. In fact, the whole kingdom had most likely heard about it by now.

Benodin finished setting out the food and headed toward the door just as Vrag entered from the back, wiping his wet face on a towel. Benodin opened the door to reveal Captain Uenk standing there with his fist raised, ready to knock. Captain Uenk stepped forward as Benodin excused herself, moving past him.

"Your Majesty," he said, his voice calm and even. "I have just received word from the Kingdom of Algron. My mother has fallen ill and requests my presence. If I may, I'd like to ask your permission to take a short leave. However," he hesitated, "if you believe I'm needed here, I can make other arrangements to see to her care."

"No, no, of course not. Though your presence is always valuable, we can get by without you for a few weeks. Go to your mother with my wishes for her safe recovery. Is there anything I need to know before you leave?"

Vrag stood with his back to Nixa while he talked to the captain, discussing minor military matters that would need to be taken care of during his absence. She hungrily glanced down at the table while she waited for them to finish their conversation, and she couldn't help but notice that a knife lay right by her plate. A sharp knife. She looked at it and then at him, not even bothering to pick it up. Such a short time ago, she would have considered taking it and using it on the king, but now, the thought held no appeal.

"So, you're not even going to try? How disappointing." Nixa's eyes shot up to catch the smirk on her ogre's face. She hadn't even heard Uenk leave.

"No, I'm not going to try. I seem to have outgrown that particular urge."

"Indeed?"

"Yes, indeed. Now sit down and eat. I'm hungry."

# Chapter 9

As Harnic was dragged from the dimly lit dungeon cell, his heart pounded in his chest. He had never been in this much trouble before, and fear gnawed at his mind.

The guards carried him through a long hallway and stopped at a heavy wooden door, which they unlocked with a large iron key. Harnic shivered at the sight and braced himself for what lay beyond.

The guards were rough and uncaring, and he stumbled as they shoved him into the room. In the flickering torchlight of the torture chamber, Harnic saw the cruel instruments of pain that lined the walls. Iron pokers, whips, knives, and other horrifying devices were there to extract the information they sought. The sight sent shivers down his spine. The guards sneered at him, their eyes filled with malice, as they fastened him onto a cold, metal table.

One of the guards, a burly man with a scarred face, leaned in close. "Where is she, dwarf?" he hissed, his hot breath making Harnic's skin crawl.

Harnic clamped his lips together tightly. The guards stepped away from him and approached a long table covered with strange tools and objects. Harnic's heart raced.

With Brulin's last whispered words echoing in his mind, Harnic stammered, "We think she... she went... to the ogre's underground city."

The guard's eyes narrowed, and he exchanged a knowing look with his comrades. "You think we're fools, dwarf? We already suspected that much."

But the guards were not done with him. They wanted to know more details about the ogre city's entrance. Harnic told them where they had been digging and what they had found. He knew it wouldn't do them any good. The humans didn't dare enter the ogre tunnels. Not if they knew what was good for them.

The guards continued their barrage of questions, asking things that Harnic couldn't possibly know. Either they thought the dwarves were in league with the ogres, or they just enjoyed torturing them and wanted an excuse to do so. Hours passed, and Harnic's body ached from the pain and exhaustion.

As time wore on, the guards grew tired of the young dwarf. Not seeing him as a threat, they stepped away momentarily to discuss their next move, convinced he wouldn't or couldn't give them any more information. This was the opportunity Harnic had been waiting for.

Dwarves don't possess magic like the elves, ogres, and goblins, but there was one thing that they did possess that made them much more formidable than humans. Dwarves were strong. Very strong. They weren't as flexible as some humans, and their height could be a disadvantage in a fight, so they had to choose their battles carefully, but lying there on the table with the guards' backs to him, Harnic dared to make a move.

He grabbed ahold of the iron restraints on his wrists, and with one mighty pull, he yanked them free from the table. The guards spun at the noise, and Harnic jumped to his feet on the table and slammed the iron shackles into the heads of the two guards closest to him. He heard the crunch of their skulls cracking as they fell to the floor.

The remaining guard pulled his sword and rushed at the dwarf. Harnic no longer had the element of surprise. He frantically ducked and dogged as the guard attacked him with the sharp blade. Jumping off the table, Harnic ran to the wall where a huge mace hung beside other weapons and implements of torture. He yanked it down with little effort and slung it around just in time to block a strike of the human's blade. Before the guard could bring the sword back around, Harnic slammed the mace into his foot. The man bent over with a cry, and Harnic swung the weapon up into his chin with such force that the guard flew backward and landed on the floor, yards away in a bloody heap.

With a lopsided grin and an excited bounce to his step, the dwarf took the key ring from the belt of one of the still, silent guards and hurried down the corridor back to the dungeon cells. He gripped the mace tightly as he reached the dungeon door. Unless they had added more guards after he left, there should only be one still there. He opened the door carefully but grimaced when a squeak rang out. Before the guard could be suspicious, Harnic threw the door open and swung the mace with all his strength. With a resounding crack, it hit the human in his knee, and the man fell to the floor with a strangled cry.

Harnic quickly finished him off and rushed to the cell where his brothers waited. With trembling hands, Harnic fumbled with the keys until he found the right one. The door creaked open, and his brothers stared at him, their eyes widening in disbelief. Finally, their surprise turned to excitement. They surrounded him, cheering and slapping him on the back. He hugged them back tightly. Brulin was the first to pull away.

"Come on!" he whispered urgently. "We need to go now!" The dwarves quickly followed him down the corridor, their footsteps echoing loudly in the empty dungeon. Brulin picked up the dead guard's sword as they passed him before leaving the dungeon, and Garroth took the dagger from his bloody boot. The others would have to wait for more guards to fall before they could arm themselves.

As they reached the end of the hallway, they heard footsteps approaching. Brulin motioned for his brothers to hide in the shadows as he and Harnic stepped forward, holding their sword and mace at the ready.

Two guards appeared. They spotted the dwarves and sneered, slowly drawing their weapons. They underestimated the men—a fatal mistake.

"Well, well, well. Look who's decided to pay us a visit," one of them said.

Brulin and Harnic didn't say a word. They charged forward, swinging their weapons with all their might. The guards tried to dodge and attack, but they weren't used to fighting dwarves. They bent awkwardly, trying to strike their shorter foes; they only managed to unbalance themselves. Before they could recover, the dwarves hit them both, sending them sprawling to the ground.

"Let's go!" Brulin shouted to his brothers.

Durfal and Ubril snatched up the guards' swords as they hurried past, and Varfid and Thondrak took their daggers.

Just then, they heard shouts from behind. Their escape had been discovered.

The dwarves hurried through the castle, trying to evade notice as the humans began searching for them. They scampered up staircases and around corners, avoiding any direct confrontation with the encroaching guards. They moved quickly and silently, staying in the shadows where possible. Now and then, they would come across a guard or two, but the dwarves' skills with their weapons and incredible strength enabled them to take down their foes without alerting any others nearby.

The dwarves continued their mad dash through the castle and into the town, their bodies aching and their hearts pounding with the urgency of their escape. They couldn't afford to be captured again, not after what they had endured in the torture chamber. Brulin led the way, his keen mind working on the fly to find the safest route out of the city.

As they neared the main gate, they could hear the commotion growing louder behind them. The alarm had been raised, and guards were converging from all directions. Their window of opportunity was rapidly closing.

Weaving between the shadows of the houses, they finally reached the city gates. The massive wooden doors stood before them, guarded by four burly soldiers. Six more stood on the top of the wall, eyes watchful and bows grasped loosely. Brulin and his brothers crouched in the shadows near the gatehouse, trying to figure out the best way past the men.

As they huddled together, hidden from view, their ears perked up when they overheard voices coming from inside the gatehouse. Through a small window, they could see two soldiers sitting at a table, drinking and conversing. At first, Brulin tuned them out, focusing on finding a way past the gate, but something in the tone of the first man's voice captured his attention.

It was heavy with remorse as he confessed to his companion, "I can't believe I let myself get caught up in this, knowing the consequences it could bring."

The other man leaned in, his face etched with concern. "Adrian, you have to tell me what's going on. What did you do?"

Adrian sighed deeply, his voice barely audible as he revealed the grim truth, "I've obtained a curse for the queen, one meant for Princess Nixa."

He had the attention of all of the dwarves at this point. They exchanged horrified glances at this revelation. Princess Nixa was in grave danger.

The other man leaned forward, his eyes widening in alarm. "A curse? You must be jesting, Adrian! The princess is harmless. Why would the queen want to curse her?"

Adrian's guilt was palpable as he spoke, "It's politics, my friend. The queen believes that by removing Princess Nixa, she can secure her own power and control over the kingdom."

The dwarves clenched their fists, their anger growing with each passing word.

The troubled man then asked a crucial question, his voice trembling, "Can the curse be broken? Is there any hope for the princess?"

Adrian hesitated, torn between loyalty to his queen and his sense of morality and guilt. Finally, he responded, "Of course. Every curse can be broken, but it's a slim chance with the princess." He shook his head sadly. "No, from what I know about her, she'll never have the curse broken."

His mind turned back to the face of the beautiful Princess of Yeatton sleeping peacefully on her bed. She would be asleep forever, too. He lifted his tankard and emptied the rest of his ale down his throat before slamming it onto the table. "Do you have any more?"

"No. We'll need to go to the tavern."

"Well, come on then."

The two men got up and stumbled to the gatehouse door.

The dwarves exchanged glances filled with a mix of despair and determination. Brulin whispered to his brothers, "We have to find Nixa and warn her, but we also need to know how to break the curse."

They observed the guards for a moment, trying to discern their patterns and weaknesses. Then, Brulin devised a plan.

Garroth, Harnic, and Ubril snuck around the gatehouse and hurried down the street back the way they had come. The clang of armor in the distance lent speed to their feet. Garroth kept going, following Adrian and the other soldier. When the shadows were deep enough, Harnic and Ubril rushed across the street and back toward the gate. Now, on the opposite side of the road, the two men walked closer to the city entrance, stumbling and bumping into each other as if they were drunk.

The eyes of the guards turned to them. All but one. He stayed vigilant. Brulin mumbled under his breath at the man's lack of distraction. Finally, Ubril, noticing the problem, tumbled onto a nearby crate, shattering it to pieces. The last guard turned to look.

Brulin and the others quickly crept from behind the gatehouse and pounced on the guards before they could cry out. The dwarves caught the men as they fell and lowered them to the ground quietly. No sound came from the guards on the wall. Hopefully, they hadn't noticed.

Brulin heaved back the bolt locking the gates and cracked them open. He and Thondrak squeezed through while Varfid, Durfal, Harnic, and Ubril moved back behind the guardhouse. When Garroth returned with news of Adrian's location, they would find him and discover how the curse could be broken, whatever it took. Outside the castle walls, Brulin and Thondrak breathed a sigh of relief, but there was no time to waste. Hurrying around to the west side of the city where the grass grew taller, they ran, hunched down, as quickly as they could away from the city.

Queen Stelia paced in her room, her steps pounding against the stone floor. Her anger gave force to her movements, removing the gracefulness that she usually employed. That insufferable girl was still on the loose, and if she was with the ogres, as all evidence seemed to show, then she could, at this very minute, be convincing them to help her take back the kingdom. The ogres had long since been considered enemies of the humans, even if they never attacked. They would probably love the excuse to go to war.

The queen grabbed a plate off a nearby table and threw it into the fireplace. The resulting crash was satisfying, but it didn't help. The problem still loomed. If she could only defeat the ogres in their own mountain, there would be no civil war. She could kill the princess in the process and tell her people that the ogres were the ones who had kidnapped and killed her, and all of her problems would disappear.

But she couldn't quite bring herself to give the order to attack. Her military didn't stand a chance, physically, against such an opponent, but everything she had ever read about the monsters said that they were a stupid people, immortal, though they were, and she could defeat stupid. She had great confidence in her strategizing. She just needed to figure out some way into the underground kingdom. If she could only sneak her men in somehow… Otherwise, she didn't see how they stood a chance. They would be easily defeated in a direct assault.

Stelia stared into the flames, her mind racing, when a movement out of the corner of her eye caught her attention. She jerked her head around. An impossibly tall and broad man stood by her balcony window. His face was fierce, with thick wrinkles crisscrossing his brow. His eyes glinted like obsidian in the firelight; his long black hair swayed softly from the wind that wafted through the open balcony doors. The man bowed his head in respect.

"Greetings, Your Majesty. I hope you will pardon this unorthodox, late-night intrusion, but I have reason to desire that my presence here goes unknown."

106

"Who are you?" Queen Stelia asked, reaching for the fireplace poker.

"Now, there's no need for that," the man replied. "I'm not here to hurt you. On the contrary, I came to offer you a deal that I very much believe you will wish to accept." He moved over beside her and gently took the fireplace poker out of her hand. Setting it back in place, he said, "I am Duke Burig from the Kingdom of Kelgrod."

"Kelgrod? But that's the ogre kingdom."

"And I am an ogre."

"You? An ogre? You look nothing like an ogre. You act nothing like an ogre."

"And what exactly does an ogre look like and act like?"

"Well, not like that." The queen waved her hand up and down at the man.

"Ah, yes," he said. "I have read your *Stories from Penningdon*, the book of tales chronicling how the human heroes and heroines always defeat the huge, ugly, stupid ogres. The illustrations are quite vivid as well, if I remember correctly."

"Are you really an ogre?"

The duke nodded.

"Then, the stories are wrong." Queen Stelia groaned in frustration and leaned her head against the fireplace mantle.

"No, I wouldn't say that," replied Burig. "At least not completely. As you can see, we are generally rather huge compared to humans. However, I would hope that you don't consider me ugly."

"And stupid?"

"Oh, yes. Ogres are quite stupid."

The queen narrowed her eyes at the man. "You don't sound stupid to me."

"That's true. But I'm only half-ogre, you see. My human half gives me an advantage in the brains department. Purebred ogres are all dull-witted imbeciles who can barely follow the simplest directions."

She stared at him askance. "If that is true, how has their society survived for as long as it has?"

Burig clasped his large hands behind his back and walked to the window. "That's a good question. The truth is the ruling class does have some measure of intelligence. Not as much as a human, mind you, but enough to ensure that they don't accidentally kill themselves. And the gemstones help. We have enough wealth in the caverns to buy food for the entire kingdom in perpetuity. So, you see, as long as the kingdom is left in peace, it can survive and even prosper, regardless of the ignorance of its citizens."

"So, if that is true, why are you here, Your Grace?"

"Because I want to be king. Of Kelgrod," he said with another bow.

"And what does that have to do with me?"

The duke began pacing the room. "I have amassed a considerable following in the city, and I have several of the guards who are loyal to me. However, I don't have quite enough to stage a successful takeover on my own. I require additional troops. You, my queen, have troops. What you don't have is a way in. As soon as your men enter the caves, they'll be taken down. The ogre warriors can see in the dark. They can hear a pin drop from a mile away. They can move faster than lightning. Your soldiers will be dead before they know what happened. Your only chance for success is to have someone on the inside. I can be that someone."

"I know ogres are strong and powerful, but surely you exaggerate their abilities somewhat."

"Perhaps, somewhat," he admitted with a wink. "But am I wrong about your chances for success?"

The queen ground her teeth. "No, you are not wrong about that. But if I help you win the throne, what's in it for me?"

"As many gems as you can carry and—Princess Nixa, if you want her."

"So, she is there. I had assumed as much."

"She is."

"She will need to die during the battle."

Duke Burig nodded. "That can be arranged."

"No, wait." Queen Stelia held up her hand. "I've changed my mind." She turned and hurried across her room. Rummaging through a dresser drawer, she pulled out a wooden box reinforced with iron bars and secured with a large padlock. She pulled a key from another drawer and opened the lid. Burig watched curiously as she pulled a shiny red apple from the box.

Brow quirked, he asked, "And what is that?"

"This, my dear duke, is my revenge."

At his puzzled look, she continued. "This apple won't kill the girl. Instead, it will trap her in an eternal 'sleep.' In all outward appearances, she will be dead." The queen shrugged. "I will see to it that she has a proper funeral befitting her station as a princess. Then I will have her placed in the royal mausoleum where she can lie for the rest of eternity, thinking over the mistakes she made in life."

"You mean she will be able to think? She will be aware of what's going on around her?"

"If my information is correct, though, there won't be much going on around her in the mausoleum, not unless you consider the scurrying of mice. I will, naturally, visit her from time to time to keep her updated with the news of my kingdom. I wouldn't want her to get too lonely and bored. I'll make sure to stop by at least once a year, maybe on her birthday. That'll be a treat for her."

"Revenge, indeed. You are quite vicious, Your Majesty."

The queen smiled as if at a great compliment. "I always treat my enemies exactly as they deserve." She placed the apple back in the box and locked the lid. "Now, when would you like this revolt of yours to take place? My men are already in position, so we can march whenever you are prepared."

"Then let's get down to business, shall we."

# Chapter 10

Nixa frowned slightly as she walked past the unfamiliar guards waiting for her outside her room that morning. She wondered where Mordak and Belnog were. Theirs were the huge, serious faces that usually greeted her each morning. She didn't comment; however, her mind was distracted by other thoughts. The strange ogres fell into step behind her as she made her way to the king's study. They had several meetings scheduled that day, but Vrag had promised her that there was a surprise waiting for her that night. She was dying of curiosity, but she would force herself to wait.

Nixa glided into Vrag's study with a smile brightening her face. She tried to keep it under control, but it seemed to have a mind of its own. If she had realized how her eyes sparkled, she would have felt even more self-conscious.

Vrag greeted her with an answering smile and motioned for her to take her seat as he turned back to the soldier giving his report. The man's words soared around the room like smoke. The princess fought to concentrate on the statements, but a large glowing crystal on Vrag's desk stole her attention. She couldn't seem to tear her eyes away from it. The shape resembled a regular crystal, but it shone and sparkled like the most intricately cut diamond. It reflected the soft glow in the room, illuminating it to twice its usual brilliance.

Nixa turned to the king in curiosity and noticed only the slightest curling of his lips. He otherwise maintained his serious expression. The infuriating man must find her astonishment amusing. She must look like a simple country bumpkin who had never seen gemstones before. With a frown, she forced her attention to the guard. Wishing he would hurry up and leave.

When the soldier finished his report and exited the room, Vrag turned to the human with a grin.

"Alright," Nixa admitted, "I've never seen anything like this before."

"Are you telling me you don't have such magnificent gems in Penningdon?"

"You know we don't," she said, hitting his arm. "I can't imagine anything else like this anywhere in the world. What is it?"

His smile grew even wider. He gently picked up the crystal and held it out to her. "Here, hold it."

She looked at him curiously before taking it. She had expected it to feel cold and heavy, but it was the opposite. The gem felt warm and light in her hand, almost like a gentle flame instead of a physical object.

"This is our Starlight Crystal," Vrag said. "It is the most treasured object of our kingdom. "Here," Vrag swept his hand over Nixa's face. "Close your eyes."

She only hesitated a moment before she complied.

"Now, feel the crystal. Let its warmth invade your body."

Nixa opened an eye and glanced at him doubtfully.

112

"Just do it," he said, covering her face again with his large hand.

Nixa concentrated on the glowing softness in her palm. She was about to ask the ogre what this was all about when she felt it, a sort of connection to the room around her. It was like she could sense where everything was. She could sense the guards stationed outside the door. She could feel the air stir with each breath she and Vrag took. Her eyes shot open.

"What was that?"

Vrag laughed. "The crystal gives anyone who holds it a deeper connection to the world around them. But it is even more powerful with the ogre royal house. Legend has it that the Starlight Crystal grants not only a connection to the kingdom but also wisdom and understanding to each king who possesses it. It is said that if the crystal is ever lost, fate has declared the king no longer fit to rule. And if someone else gains the crystal, they are the rightful ruler of the kingdom."

"Do you have to hold it all the time for it to work?"

Vrag reached for the stone, and Nixa reluctantly handed it back. Her hand felt colder without it.

"No," he replied, "but it is certainly stronger when we do. Many times, during war or famine or other troubled days, kings have carried the crystal around as they attended meetings and made important decisions. But once a king has connected to it, he can draw on its power from a distance. At least, until someone else connects to it."

"Only kings? What about queens?"

"Ogre kingdoms don't have queens, except for the wives of the kings, and they don't connect to the stone."

Nixa frowned. However, it wasn't so different in her kingdom. Penningdon had never had a queen rule alone, after all, but there was no law against it. She still had a small hope that she would be the first.

Vrag lifted his hand to pat her head but paused when he remembered their conversation. Instead, he ran his fingers through her hair. She was beginning to enjoy that sensation more and more when a thought suddenly pushed itself to the forefront of her mind.

"Is there a queen? Of Kelgrod, I mean. Are you married?" She hadn't heard of any wife, but now that she thought of it, she hadn't seen any ogre ladies around the castle at all.

Vrag's eyelids lowered seductively, and Nixa's stomach fluttered.

"Why do you ask?" His voice was low. Intense.

Nixa cleared her throat and looked away. She reached out and ran her fingers over the Starlight Crystal he had set back in its holder.

"No reason." She couldn't bring herself to meet his eyes. "I just realized I haven't seen any ogre ladies around."

Vrag humphed. "That is intentional. This is a bachelor establishment, and I don't like having a swarm of ladies constantly flying around me like mosquitos, endlessly vying for my attention."

Nixa raised her brows and grinned. "Really? I would think that most men would like that."

The king snorted. "Not when all they want is a crown."

Nixa felt her cheeks warm as her traitorous eyes ran up and down his body. "I don't think that's all they want," she murmured.

Vrag leaned in close, his body invading her space like a granite wall. His eyes blazed with deep emotion. Nixa's breath hitched in her throat. Her heart beat against her chest. She gripped the arms of her chair so tightly her knuckles were white. She instinctively leaned back, but he followed her until the back of the chair stopped her progress.

Vrag continued leaning in until his lips were mere inches from her ear. So close his breath tickled her cheek when he spoke.

"And what else would they want?" The deep guttural whisper ignited a fire in her belly. He reached up and brushed her hair away from her neck. His lips moved closer.

Just then, someone loudly cleared their throat, and Nixa's eyes shot over to the man standing before the desk. She hadn't even heard him come in.

Vrag growled but didn't move away. Nixa shut her eyes tightly as he continued to play with her hair, his face only inches from hers.

"What do you want, Thronig?"

"I have my report that you requested on the new trade routes."

With a sigh, the king slowly leaned away. He held out his hand, and the ogre gave him a stack of papers. Nixa still didn't move as Vrag flipped through them. She only slightly began to relax as the two men discussed the information in the report. It wasn't until Thronig left that she managed to get her body entirely under control. Outwardly, she appeared to be a perfectly composed princess, but inwardly, she was a cyclone. A raging fire. A tumult of emotions ready to explode.

She held her breath when Thronig walked out the door, and Vrag turned toward her again, but he didn't have an opportunity to do anything before another ogre entered the room.

Thankfully.

Unfortunately.

To Nixa's relief, to her disappointment, there was a steady stream of meetings for the rest of the day. After the last man left, Vrag turned to her, cupped the back of her head with his hand, and leaned in to kiss her forehead. Then he lifted her out of the chair by her arms and gave her a gentle push toward the door.

"Hurry back to your chambers. Benodin has a surprise for you that's been eating her alive for days."

Nixa grabbed the doorknob and jerked the door open. Her brain felt like mush as she practically fled the room. Whether she ran *to* the surprise or *from* the king, she couldn't say, but she didn't stop until she reached the safety of her chambers.

Garroth quietly joined his brothers, still waiting behind the guardhouse. "He's gone into a tavern. Come on," he said, moving cautiously back down the street.

The dwarves took up a position in an alleyway across from the tavern. The store beside them had stacked empty barrels in the narrow space, and the men hid behind them, thankful for the cover. Squatting in muck of questionable origin that marred the ground, they waited.

"Where are we going to question him when we catch him?" Ubril whispered. "It needs to be somewhere private, so we can...question him effectively."

The brothers looked at each other, considering.

"He's a soldier, isn't he?" asked Durfal.

Nods and shrugs were the only response.

"Well, if he is, he'll probably return to the castle barracks when he's finished there," Durfal continued. "I'll head in that direction and see if I can find any good temporary accommodations along the way."

"That's a good idea," said Varfid. "I'll go with you."

They disappeared into the darkness while the others continued to wait.

Legs and thighs aching from the uncomfortable position, Garroth considered sitting on a nearby box, but the rotten wood appeared too weak to hold his weight, and he didn't relish the thought of getting his trousers covered in whatever was squishing under his boots. He wrinkled his nose at the smell of urine, rotting food, and vomit that permeated the air so close to the tavern. The sounds of loud, off-key singing erupted from the building across the street, drowning out the scurry of mice that had been their only music.

Still, they waited. Garroth had to adjust his position when his legs began falling asleep, and he heard a few of the others moving around as well. The singing morphed into angry shouts that ended in a dull thump and laughter. Then, another raunchy drinking song filled the air. Durfal and Varfid returned and squatted down beside Garroth.

"We found the perfect spot," Durfal said, a wide grin spreading his beard.

"We've got it all set up and ready for him," added Varfid.

Garroth nodded. "Let's just hope that's the path he takes."

A shout rang out from inside the tavern, followed by laughter and more shouting. Finally, a loud crash came from within the building. Garroth heard the sound of breaking glass and tensed. Then, as if in slow motion, Adrian staggered out into the night with an unsteady gait. He wobbled around for a minute before making his way down the street. He weaved about with his arms held up in a wild gesture as if conducting some grand orchestra.

The dwarves waited until he had gone around the corner before they emerged from their hiding place and began to follow him.

Garroth moved swiftly but not too close so as not to startle Adrian or draw undue attention to them. Now and then, Adrian stopped, hunched over as if trying to remember which way he was going, then picked himself up again and continued on his way. His stumbling gait was unsteady, and his eyes rolled wildly in their sockets. He mumbled something incoherently with every step.

Garroth couldn't help but feel a small bit of pity for the man. He must be quite upset about something to allow himself to get to that state. But it was good news for them. Drunk as he was, it might be easier to get the information they wanted. As long as he didn't pass out first, that is.

Durfal motioned to an alleyway on the left, and the dwarves quickly joined Adrian. Garroth got his attention when they reached him, and the drunk man looked down at him curiously.

"Hey there"

"Hi," replied Garroth, his nose wrinkling at the stench of ale emanating from the man.

"You're dwarves," said Adrian, his words slurring almost beyond recognition.

"Yes, we are."

"Hi, dwarves."

"Hi. Would you like some more ale?" asked Garroth.

"Dwarf's ale?"

"Yes, dwarf ale."

"Sure." He stretched the word out and almost tripped over his own feet as he turned around in a circle. "Where's it?"

"It's over here. Follow us." Durfal led them to an old warehouse that appeared to be abandoned. The walls looked like they would fall at the slightest provocation, and the door barely hung on its hinges, but it still closed securely enough behind them.

Adrian stumbled in, and the dwarves led him toward a low table in the middle of the room.

The man mumbled to himself as he lurched forward another few steps before he stumbled and nearly fell into a nearby crate. "Strange tavern. Where's the ale? Is't invisible ale?"

"Yes," Garroth said, grabbing his arm and pulling him to the table. "It's invisible, magic dwarf ale."

Adrian stopped and gasped. "Will's it make me invisible, too?"

"Do you want to be invisible?"

Adrian grimaced. "Will my mind go invisible? And my thoughts?"

"Yes, it will make your thoughts invisible."

"Then, yes. I don't want to see my thoughts," he said as he sat on the table. "My thoughts are bad."

"Why are your thoughts bad?" asked Ubril, pushing the taller man's legs onto the table so he would lie down.

Adrian put his finger against his lips. "Shh. Don't tell nobody. I did something bad," he said, sitting up and trying to cross his legs.

"What did you do?" asked Garroth.

Adrian shook his head violently and wagged his finger at them. "Nope, nope, nope, nope. I can't tell. The queen will be mad if I tell." He leaned down toward them and whispered conspiratorially. "She's gonna curse the princess, and I helped her."

"How will the queen curse the princess?" asked Garroth.

Adrian shot up straight and stared at the man. "How you know 'bout the curse?"

Garroth ground his teeth together in frustration. "I'm a dwarf," he said. "We know everything."

"Really? That's awesome. Can I know everything?"

"Sure, if you answer my questions, I'll give you magic so you can know everything."

"Wow! Ugh. Wait a minute." Adrian turned around and vomited off the side of the table. He wiped his mouth on his sleeve and turned back to Garroth. "What do you want to ask?" he replied as though the conversation hadn't been interrupted, and a stench wasn't rising from the ground.

Garroth found his patience almost gone. He clenched his fists and stepped forward, ready to punch the man.

Varfid stopped him with his question. "How is the princess going to be cursed?"

"It's a fruit. An apple. S'how she's going to do it. Give the girl an apple."

"How can the curse be broken?" Varfid asked.

Adrian leaned his head back and wailed. "It can't! She don't love me. I tried to break it. I tried." He bent down and grabbed Garroth's shirt. He stared into his eyes. "You believe me? I loved her. I tried to break the curse, but she didn't love me."

Garroth reached up and removed the man's hands. He cast a puzzled glance at his brothers. "Princess Nixa doesn't love you?"

"No, not Princess Nixa. Princess Elora."

"The Yeatton princess?" asked Ubril, confused.

Suddenly, Garroth understood. "You were in love with the Princess of Yeatton."

Adrian nodded sadly.

"But she didn't love you because you are a horrible person," said Ubril, trying a new tactic.

"I'm horrible." Adrian swayed on the table, and his eyes began to close.

"No, no. Stay awake," said Garroth urgently. "If you want the invisible ale, tell us how to break the curse. You said you couldn't break it because she didn't love you. Could you have broken it if she did?"

Adrian made kissing motions and opened his arms as if embracing someone. "I kissed her. But she didn't love me. She stayed sleeping."

"So, true love's kiss will break the curse?" asked Garroth.

Adrian continued kissing the air.

Ubril grabbed the man's leg and shook it. "Will true love's kiss break the curse?"

Adrian nodded, hugging himself tightly. "True love's kiss. The only way she'll wake up. But she didn't love me." He broke down into sobs and fell over onto his side, almost sliding off the table. The dwarves ignored him.

"Do you think that's it?" asked Garroth.

"It sounds like it," said Varfid. "At least, that's what he thinks."

The men turned back to look at the pathetic human. His eyes had shut, and snores shook his body.

"Regardless, that's all we're going to get out of him," said Varfid.

"Does Nixa love anyone?" asked Harnic.

The brothers shared a hopeless glance.

"Come on," said Garroth. "We might be able to reach her before she eats the apple. Then, it wouldn't matter."

They rushed out of the room, leaving Adrian to his drunken dreams.

As soon as they stepped out of the old warehouse, the brothers heard the sound of hooves pounding on the street nearby. They hugged the buildings and cautiously made their way down the alley. Soldiers filled the road, heading toward the gate.

The dwarves waited until they had passed and carefully followed, staying in the darkness of the shadows as much as possible. They had to stop a block away from the gate. Men with torches filled the street. They didn't dare risk going any closer.

One of the men rode to the front of the group and held his torch high. "There are seven of them armed with stolen weapons. Don't let their size fool you. They are incredibly strong and well-trained. They've already killed several guards in the castle. Don't bother taking prisoners. The queen is finished with them. Kill them all. Move out."

Garroth and the others watched the men leave. They needed to get out the gate somehow, or they would be stuck inside the city walls. The gate guards would be much more diligent now. Or would they? If they thought the dwarves had already escaped, would they let down their guard? Regardless, they had to get out of the city. They had to reach Nixa. There wasn't much time.

# Chapter 11

The Moonlight Masque was unlike any ball Nixa had ever attended, and she had attended plenty. She didn't know how Benodin had managed to keep it a secret from her for so long. And her dress was magnificent! It shimmered in the light of the moonstones. A beautiful shade of midnight blue, with intricate ivory embroidery and sparkling moonstone accents that glittered like stars in a night sky, the delicate fabric draped over her body like liquid silver. She adjusted her moonstone mask as she entered the elaborate ballroom on Vrag's arm.

"Presenting His Majesty, King Vrag Nerig Orin, Ruler of Kelgrod. And his human, Princess Nixa of Penningdon.

Nixa resisted the urge to glare at the herald. He hadn't even bothered to ask her her full name. Well, it didn't matter. At least he had announced her. From what she understood, that wasn't a common practice with pets. Perhaps the ogres were finally beginning to see her as more than a pet.

The princess stood as regally as the king. She would show them that human royalty was just as good as ogre royalty. Her eyes swept the room as everyone bowed and curtseyed before them. Well, before Vrag.

She searched their faces as they rose to see what they thought of her. It wasn't too difficult to read the expressions of the ogre ladies. Hatred and jealousy radiated off them in waves. Just then, she was glad that there weren't any ogre ladies living in the castle. She wouldn't want to have to put up with this every day.

It was then that she realized how truly different things were there. She was sure that many, if not most, of the ladies of her own court hated her or were, at least, jealous of her. Yet, it had never bothered her there. There, she'd held a position of power. Such things, such people, were beneath her. Here, though, she held no power but what the king chose to give her. For the first time in her life, she was vulnerable in court. She would have to be careful tonight.

Before she could think any more on it, Vrag swept her up in his arms and onto the dancefloor. A giggle burst from her lips before she could stop it, and he grinned in response. She placed one hand on his bicep and the other in his large palm as he pulled her close. She wasn't familiar with ogre customs, but he held her too tightly for human propriety, though she didn't complain.

His strong hand rested firmly on her waist, his touch gentle yet assertive, guiding her through the intricate steps of the dance. The subtle pressure of his fingers sent shivers down her spine. She couldn't help but feel drawn to him. His mask concealed his features, but his eyes, visible behind the intricate carvings, seemed to hold a magnetic allure.

She barely noticed the light reflecting off the elaborately carved moonstone masks everyone wore, the gentle, soft white glow emanating from moonstone lanterns, the beautiful gowns and the elegant suits the guests sported, the deep bass music filling the air, the sparkle of the Starlight Crystal sitting on a pedestal before his throne.

Vrag's body, his musky scent, his very essence filled her senses. His broad chest and handsome face were all she saw. His muscular bicep and warm hands were all she felt. His breath was all she heard. And she breathed him in with each inhale. Her eyes lingered on his lips, and for just a moment, she remembered how he had tasted when he had stolen a kiss.

When her eyes found their way back to his, it was all she could do to keep dancing. They were dark and stormy. Filled with a passion she tried to deny in herself. But couldn't. She wanted nothing more than to stand in his arms and finish what they had started in his office. That thought jerked her back to reality, and her eyes darted around the room.

Had anyone seen? Were they behaving inappropriately?

Vrag's chuckle was deep, husky. Almost forced.

"Perhaps we should sit out the next dance," he said when the music stopped.

The tension eased, and her heart started again as he led her off the dance floor and to the refreshment area.

Nixa didn't think she could eat a bite until she smelled the delicious aromas wafting up from the table. She filled a small plate and took a glass of some unfamiliar sweet drink. Vrag had said it was safe, and she trusted him. Surprisingly.

Nibbling on her snacks and sipping the delicious liquid, she followed the king around the room as he greeted his subjects. He introduced her to everyone he stopped to talk to. Not as his pet. Not as the human. As Princess Nixa of the Kingdom of Penningdon.

She beamed. A feeling of warmth spread through her at this sign of respect. He was declaring to his court that she was a person and that he expected them to treat her as such.

The glares she received from the ladies, behind his back, of course, didn't diminish, but at least no one dared criticize her outright. Many of the men of the court even seemed amused at the situation. They played along as if at a great joke, bowing elegantly over her hand and greeting her effusively.

Some of the ogre nobles even seemed to welcome her presence, their eyes traveling back and forth between her and their king. *Could they be thinking of the benefits of an alliance?* thought Nixa. It would solve many problems. Surely, he would help her take back her kingdom if they formed an alliance. Or, if it were a marriage alliance, she thought with a blush, she wouldn't need to take back her kingdom. Or she could, and they could rule over both.

One of the noblemen interrupted her thoughts by asking her to dance. Nixa gave Vrag a quick glance. The hard glint in his eyes revealed his displeasure, but if their court were anything like hers, she couldn't refuse without consequences. Besides, this was something she was good at: dancing and entrancing men.

"Of course, Lord Gronk. It would be my pleasure," she said, handing her plate and glass to a nearby servant and taking the offered hand.

They moved to the dance floor and glided across the smooth stone to the rhythms of the music. He stood a little shorter than Vrang, so she could almost reach his shoulder. Almost. She gripped the top of his bicep with one hand and placed the other in his. Why were all these ogres so freakishly tall?

Gronk's movements were surprisingly light, though, considering his immense size, and he moved with a grace that belied his appearance.

"So, what do you think of our underground community, princess? It's quite different from the world above, I imagine," he said.

Nixa replied, "It's fascinating. Your city is a hidden treasure, and the Moonstone Masquerade is unlike any ball I've ever attended. I'm in awe of the beauty and magic that surrounds us."

Gronk lifted her and spun her in the pattern of the dance, his mask hiding any hint of emotion, but his eyes held a spark of curiosity. "It's good to hear that you appreciate it. Our people take great pride in our way of life. Tell me, what's the world above like? What are the humans like in your realm?"

Pleased at his interest, Nixa spoke of her own world as they moved across the dance floor, describing the human kingdoms, the lush landscapes, and the bustling cities. Gronk listened intently, seemingly intrigued by the images she painted in his mind.

As the music ended, Gronk led her between the larger dancers toward the side of the room, "Princess Nixa, I'm glad we had this opportunity to talk. It's rare for us to interact with outsiders, and your perspective has been enlightening."

Nixa smiled. "The pleasure was mine, Lord Gronk."

With a bow, the nobleman wandered away. Nixa caught Vrag's gaze and headed to him, but before she had managed more than a couple of steps, she felt a hand on her shoulder and turned.

Another ogre stood behind her. With a deep and respectful bow, he said, "Allow me to introduce myself, Your Highness. I am Count Thrain. Might I humbly request the pleasure of a dance with you this evening?"

Nixa nodded and took his hand.

"I can't help but be curious how you find our world compared to yours. Does it seem exotic to you or too dark and dreary?"

Nixa smiled. Had none of these ogres interacted with humans before? They all seemed so curious about her. Or was that because she was the first human there who was treated as a real person and not some animal relegated to the background. Whatever the reason, she didn't mind appeasing their curiosity. Anything to help them see her as an equal.

She replied with genuine enthusiasm, "Oh, definitely exotic. The entire underground city is a marvel. Your culture's respect for the mountain and your ability to live in harmony with it is something I find truly remarkable."

Thrain's eyes revealed a hint of pride. "We take great pride in our connection to the underground. It's a testament to our history and the strength of our people. We've always found beauty in the depths."

Nixa was in her element. She knew how to shmooze with men of the court. She asked all the right questions and said all the right things. She even surprised herself when she realized she meant every word of it. As the dance ended, Thrain left her with another deep bow.

"Princess Nixa, your presence has added a unique spark to our Moonstone Masquerade, much like the moonstones themselves. Thank you for gracing us with your company this evening."

Nixa curtsied gracefully even though her rank didn't require it. "The pleasure was mine, Count Thrain. I'm grateful for this opportunity to share in your culture."

This time, when she left the dance floor, Vrag was right there waiting for her. Another ogre hurried over to her from the side of the room, but when the king turned to him and growled, he quickly redirected his steps to another lady. Without a word, Vrag grabbed her hand, tucked it into his arm, and escorted her from the room.

"Where are we going?" Nixa asked, feeling the seeds of unease.

"You looked tired. I thought you might enjoy a break from the dancing."

Nixa smirked but didn't say anything. She wasn't the least bit tired, and she was pretty sure Vrag knew it.

"But where are we going?" She glanced back over her shoulder at the open doors of the ballroom. "Won't people notice our absence and comment on it."

"Not at all," he replied gruffly. "Look around." He waved his hand at the hallway, indicating the various alcoves and benches filled with ogres sitting and talking. Many of the guests were taking the opportunity to spend some time in more private settings.

"Oh."

"Where did you think I was taking you?" he asked, humor warring with something more intense in his voice.

Nixa glanced up at his face and then quickly looked away, her cheeks turning almost as red as her cherry lips.

"Nowhere. I was just curious."

Vrag stopped and leaned down toward her. "Don't worry, my little pet," he whispered, "I have a feeling that one of these days soon, I'm going to take you exactly where you're thinking of right now."

Nixa squeaked, and he chuckled as he started walking again, pulling her along with him.

"But right now, I thought you might enjoy seeing the gardens. It is a popular place for couples to go to escape the heat of the ballroom. And it was hot in there, wasn't it?"

Yes, it was hot in there. And it was getting hot out here as well, but she wouldn't admit it to him, not when he had that smug look on his face. She just huffed and followed him along.

Nixa's breath caught as they entered the conservatory. The garden was a hidden oasis, a testament to the ingenuity and magic of the ogres. Rows of exotic flowers, their petals in various shades of blues and purples, reached toward the soft light of the blue disks floating above and the moonstone lanterns sitting around. A sweet, delicate fragrance filled the air, and a gentle breeze, with mysterious origins, fanned her face.

"It's breathtaking. I had no idea such a vibrant garden could exist underground." Nixa ran her fingers over the soft petals of an unfamiliar flower.

Vrag nodded, his eyes filled with pride. "We have nurtured this garden for generations. Ogres have an excellent ability to adapt and create beauty in unexpected places."

He took her arm again, and they strolled along the winding paths. Vrag spoke of the various flowers and their significance to the ogre culture, his deep voice resonating in the space.

"These are the Moonlit Lilies," he explained, his eyes flickering with a soft glow as he gestured to a cluster of delicate, pale blue blossoms. Nixa listened attentively, her eyes tracing the contours of the unique flower.

"They're extraordinary."

"The moonstones power not only the enchanting lights but also our magic. They're the lifeblood of our city, and they allow us to thrive in this subterranean world. These flowers represent that relationship. We believe that by respecting the earth and all its wonders, we can create a world that thrives in balance with nature."

This was a side of the king she hadn't often seen. He was very professional when tending to business matters and had been playful, or otherwise, when dealing with her, but a sense of ownership and pride radiated off him as he told her of his culture, almost as if he wanted her to feel the same love for it as he did.

This walk might have started as a way to distract themselves from more intense, inappropriate thoughts, but it was turning out to be quite special. If they ever did consider an alliance between their two kingdoms, it would be helpful to know things like this about his culture. She smiled as she watched the animation on his face when he spoke of his people and his land. She liked this side of him, too.

"Your world is so different from mine," said Nixa, "yet there's a profound beauty in its uniqueness."

Vrag looked deeply into her eyes. "And your presence has added a new layer of enchantment and beauty."

Nixa resisted the urge to fan herself as they continued their leisurely walk through the garden, but she did allow herself to sink into the magic of the moment. The garden's beauty, the soft glow of the moonstones, and the connection they shared made it a night she would never forget.

It was late when Nixa and Vrag finally said their goodnights. They had eventually returned to the ballroom, and she had danced with other members of the court. King Vrag had danced with some of the other ladies, too, managing to diffuse the jealous tension in the room to a small degree. But the last dance, they danced together.

Nixa hummed to herself and waltzed around her small room when they returned to his chambers. Benodin kept chuckling as she helped the princess get ready for bed. Nixa fell asleep to the memory of his strong arms holding her and his heart beating against her ear.

Duke Burig's guards headed into the city. Lights and music emanated from the castle as the nobles danced at the Moonlight Masquerade. A few ogres wandered about the town in the commoner's quarter, seeing to their individual tasks, but most of them had already gone home for the night. The guards approached a small house, and one knocked on the door.

The young woman inside groaned at the interruption and set down the book she had been reading. She pushed herself out of her chair and shuffled towards the door, opening it cautiously. She stepped back when she saw the uniforms of the ogres.

"What is it?" she asked with a quiver in her voice. "Has something happened at the castle? Are Benodin and father alright?"

The ogres did not answer her, instead pushing past her into the house without warning. She watched them with worried eyes. The two guards quickly glanced around to ensure no one else was there. When they saw they were alone, they exchanged glances before one stepped forward and grabbed her arm.

"What are you doing?" she cried, trying to pull away from the ogre's grip.

"Quiet, woman," the guard growled, his grip tightening. "We have orders from Duke Burig."

The woman's eyes widened in fear. "What does he want from me?"

"That's none of your business," the first guard spat. "Now, come with us."

The woman tried to resist, but the ogre's grip was too tight. They dragged her out the back door of the house and down the deserted back alleys towards the castle.

She tried to scream, but the ogre covered her mouth and held her tightly.

"Quiet," he growled. "You wouldn't want to get seriously injured before we arrive at our destination, would you?"

The woman's eyes widened in fear, and she closed her mouth.

The two guards led their captive down a shadowy side street into a secret tunnel. The darkness was thick, but with their ogre eyes, they had no difficulty navigating through the narrow passageways. Eventually, they reached a large cavern where an army of human soldiers waited.

Queen Stelia stood at their head, her gaze stern and determined. She nodded in acknowledgment when she saw the two guards.

"Put out your torches and follow us," said one of the ogres.

With a wave of her hand, Queen Stelia signaled for her troops to begin marching forward.

The ogres led the troops down secret tunnel after secret tunnel, pulling their prisoner behind them. Their path twisted and turned to such a degree that the humans would never be able to find their way out on their own. They occasionally reentered the dim alleyways of the town only to dive back into another dark cave tunnel farther down the road.

The ogre guards didn't allow the humans to carry any lights for fear of being seen. So, Queen Stelia and her soldiers were forced to hold onto each other in a long line as they made their way through the darkness, like schoolchildren following their teachers. The helplessness of the situation sent a shudder down her spine. Had she made the right decision? And who was the female ogre captive they pulled along with them? Clearly, the duke hadn't told her everything. Could she trust him, or were they leading her into a trap? She had no choice but to continue following the men and hope for the best, but as they descended deeper and deeper into the tunnels, she could feel her stomach twist in fear.

Finally, they reached a small wooden door blocking the cave passage. One of the guards took out a key, unlocked the door, and swung it open. With a finger to his lips and a knife to the ogre girl's neck in warning, he led his entourage into a large cavern. Shelves lined with canned goods filled the space so that the human troops had to squeeze together for them all to fit.

One of the ogre guards cautiously cracked open a door on the other side of the room and listened. When he heard no movement, he slowly eased into the hallway and disappeared. Several minutes later, he returned, dragging a body dressed in servant's attire.

"The way's clear now," he said quietly. He pulled the limp body into a shadowy corner. The ogre captive stared in horror as he casually threw it behind some crates and walked away.

He motioned for the others to follow and led them into the silent hall. Apparently, everyone else was either in the kitchen or at the ball, dancing, serving, or watching the guests. The group managed to reach the guard's training room in the basement without seeing another soul.

Duke Burig, himself, met them there. His presence reassured the queen somewhat, though she didn't like feeling trapped. He motioned for his guards to take their prisoner away and invited Stelia to join him as he sat at one of the rough tables. The human soldiers began setting up a temporary camp, thankful for the hovering blue lights that lent some welcome illumination to the space.

Now, they would rest. If all went according to plan, the following day would bring them both victory and the prizes they so longed for.

# Chapter 12

The next morning, Nixa dressed and prepared for the day as usual, but when she left her room, instead of heading in the direction of the king's office, her new guards led her down the hallway that led to her old chambers.

"What's going on?" she asked, glancing around nervously.

"King Vrag requested that you meet him in your old rooms this morning," replied one of the guards gruffly.

Nixa felt a chill run through her. Something wasn't right. "Where's Mordak and Belnog?" She attempted to make her voice casual when she asked about her old guards, but some of her nervousness must have seeped through because the men picked up the pace.

"They were sent off on a special assignment," one of them replied.

"Oh." Nixa clasped her hands nervously in front of her as she followed them.

When they reached her old bedroom, the guards opened the door and stood to the side for her to enter.

Nixa walked in and looked around the room in confusion. No one was there. What did this mean?

The two ogre guards motioned for Nixa to sit on the bed. One of them approached and held out a gold collar.

The same gold collar Vrag had first put on her or one just like it. Nixa gasped and jerked away from him, but the other guard had come up behind her. He grabbed her head between his huge, strong hands and held it still while the other guard clasped and secured the collar around her neck.

"What are you doing?" she asked frantically. "King Vrag didn't order this! He wouldn't!"

The guards just laughed and walked out the door, locking it behind them.

A few moments later, Duke Burig arrived at the king's office, followed by two of his guards. Vrag was seated in his chair behind the wide desk, impatiently tapping his fingers.

"Where is Nixa?" he scowled. "She should be here by now."

Burig stepped forward and cleared his throat. "I'm afraid the princess won't be joining us this morning," he said quietly. He reached into his pocket and pulled out an ornate mirror, waving his hand over it as he spoke.

The king leaned forward to see the image in the mirror—Nixa sitting on her bed in her bedroom with the gold collar around her neck.

"What is this?" Vrag demanded angrily, jumping up from his seat.

Burig spoke again in a low voice so the guards outside the door couldn't hear him. "I can control this collar remotely," he said, "and if you want her back unharmed, then you'll do as I say."

138

The king gritted his teeth in frustration. "What do you want?"

"I want you to give me the Starlight Crystal," the duke said confidently.

Vrag scoffed. "I'll never surrender that to the likes of you." He waved his hand in the air. "The human's only a pet. Your threat holds no weight."

"Then you leave me no choice." Burig gestured to his guards, who pulled out their swords and pointed them threateningly at the king.

"Now." He laid the mirror on Vrag's desk. "Watch as your little human pet dies."

Once again, he waved his hand over the mirror, and Nixa gasped. Her hand flew to her neck, desperately grasping the collar. Her eyes flew open wide, and she struggled to breathe as the gold restraint began to choke her.

Vrag's throat closed, and his chest felt like a boulder crushed it. A growl burst out between his tightly pressed lips. "Stop! I'll give you the blasted crystal."

Immediately, the image of Nixa relaxed as she sucked in deep breaths. Duke Burig picked up the mirror and hid it away in the folds of his cloak. He motioned toward the door.

"Lead the way," he said, "but don't forget. I can activate the collar at any time from any location. It cannot be removed except by me, and I have spelled it to kill her if anything unfortunate happens to me."

Vrag pushed himself up from his chair and stomped over to the door. Burig stopped him before he opened it.

"I think it is probably for the best if your guards don't suspect anything unusual is happening, don't you," he said sweetly. Vrag glared at him, but before he opened the door, he took a deep breath and schooled his features.

They made their way through the castle, down seldom-used hallways and stairs, through twisting passages etched in shadows, and into an ancient corridor with arched ceilings and thick stone walls deep in the heart of the castle. Finally, they came to a large room guarded by two more ogres. The two guards standing outside the room immediately snapped to attention when they saw their liege, their eyes staring straight ahead.

Vrag stepped into the room with a heavy heart. It was the room where he kept the kingdom's most prized possession—the famed Starlight Crystal. He had sworn to protect it with his life, but now, here he was, about to hand it over to a duke who had proven himself over the years to be ruthless and manipulative. Would the people believe the old stories about the crystal? Would Burig be able to take the kingdom from him with it?

Burig seemed to sense Vrag's hesitation and stepped further into the room. "Well? Will you give me my prize, or shall I take it by force?" He glared at Vrag through narrowed eyes, daring him to refuse. Vrag knew that he had no choice in this matter; if he refused, then Nixa would surely die. He clenched his fists in frustration before nodding silently and turning away from Burig.

A pedestal stood in the middle of the chamber with the shimmering crystal resting on top. Vrag silently motioned for his guards to stay back while he stepped forward and took the crystal from its perch. He reluctantly held it out to Burig. The duke's eyes widened at its beauty, and he reached out to touch it. A chill ran up his spine as he felt its power humming through his fingertips.

"Ahh," breathed Burig reverently, "I have waited so long for this day."

He gently took the crystal from the king and cradled it carefully in both hands as if it were made of glass before tucking it away inside his cloak with a satisfied smirk.

"Thank you, King Vrag," said Burig smugly as he made his way out of the room. "You have been most generous."

With a curt nod, he signaled one of his men, who let out a loud whistle. A door down the hall flew open, and human soldiers poured into the room, swords drawn. Vrag whipped his sword from the scabbard he always wore around his waist and met the onslaught head on. A fierce and chaotic battle erupted as King Vrag and his loyal ogre guards clashed with Duke Burig's men.

Vrag's world narrowed to a fevered tunnel of action and reaction. His massive frame moved with a primal grace that defied his size. Every swing of his sword was a brutal proclamation of power, capable of slicing through a man's armor and bones. His blows sent humans and rival ogres alike sprawling, but the numbers against him were overwhelming. His own guards, equally valiant, fought with all their might. Blood and sweat mingled as they defended their king.

His senses were alive with the adrenaline surging through his veins. His bellowing roars echoed through the chamber, a challenge and a battle cry that struck terror into the hearts of his foes. His eyes scanned the frenzied melee as he sought out the most immediate threats.

As humans and rival ogres rushed him, Vrag met them head-on, his sword swinging with a destructive force. Screams and cries of agony filled his ears. The satisfaction of those moments was visceral.

Yet, for all his might and ferocity, the odds were against him. His assailants were relentless. For every foe they dispatched, it seemed another two took their place. The humans, driven by Duke Burig's command, fought with a desperate determination that Vrag had not anticipated. More and more of them swarmed around him.

As the battle raged on, the room's once pristine floors were stained with the blood of the fallen. Vrag's breath came in heavy, laborious gasps. His once unrelenting movements grew sluggish. The taste of blood mingled with the saltiness of his sweat on his lips, and the aching in his limbs grew more pronounced.

He watched as his guards, too, began to tire, their weary expressions mirroring his own. Despite their resilience, the weight of sheer numbers was slowly wearing them down, pushing them to their limits.

With each passing moment, it became painfully clear that victory was slipping from their grasp. They were vastly outnumbered, and their once fierce defense was faltering. The humans and Burig's guards pressed forward relentlessly, their combined might proving too great.

In the end, there was no other choice. As the weight of their impending defeat bore down upon them, Vrag and his guards were forced to concede. Kneeling on the ground with a dozen swords pointed at his neck, Vrag felt the cold metal of restraints encircling his wrists as Burig's men clamped him in irons.

"Take him to the dungeons," he said. "I'll be along to question him in a little while."

"Do you think this is all it will require for you to take over the kingdom?" Vrag asked with a sneer as the men pulled him to his feet.

"I have the crystal, and you will conveniently disappear. You have never birthed an heir, and I am a duke of the realm. I don't foresee any problems."

"Then you are a fool and deserve the painful death you have coming."

Burig just laughed and motioned for his men to take the prisoners away. He turned and headed upstairs to meet the queen and tell her of their victory, leaving a hallway full of dead bodies behind.

Benodin's hands shook as she clasped her bundle to her chest. Sweat beaded on her brow even as a shiver wracked her body. But she put on a smile and stepped past the guards into the princess's chamber.

"Benodin!" Nixa jumped off the bed and rushed to the lady's maid.

Benodin practically threw her bundle on the table and hurried to embrace the princess.

"Are you alright?" she asked.

Nixa nodded, raising her hand to touch the golden collar.

Benodin pulled the girl over to the table and gently pushed her into a chair. She poured her a glass of water from the pitcher on the table and handed it to her. Nixa took a sip.

"Where's Vrag?" she asked. "Why did he do this to me?"

Benodin hesitated. "I don't think he did."

"What do you mean?"

Benodin glanced over her shoulder at the door. "There are new guards out there, and nobody seems to know where the king is."

Nixa sat up straighter. "What do you mean?"

"I think," Benodin pursed her lips. "I think Duke Burig has taken over."

"How's that possible? Wouldn't we have heard fighting? Vrag wouldn't just let him take over without a fight."

Benodin's gaze dropped to Nixa's collar. "No, but he could have been threatened or tricked somehow."

Nixa again raised her hand to her neck. "You think Burig's the one responsible for this? But... Vrag wouldn't care if he threatened me. I'm only his pet."

Benodin tilted her head and stared at Nixa intently. "You know better than that. He cares for you."

Nixa's face grew warm, and her heart skipped a beat. "Do you really think so?" she asked, her voice barely above a whisper. She shook her head, dismissing the thought and the thrill that went along with it. "Be that as it may, he's not the kind of man to turn over the kingdom to someone like Burig, not even to save someone he cares about. Is he?"

Benodin shrugged. "Who can say? I don't think he's ever really cared deeply for anyone before. I don't know what he'd be willing to do. But even if he didn't trade the kingdom for you, you could have been used to lure him into a trap. Either way, I know he isn't the one who put the collar back on you. He wouldn't do that."

"Why do you think it's the duke?"

Benodin's eyes wandered to the bundle before she forced them back to the princess.

"I don't know." She walked over to the dressing table and began fiddling with the items lying there.

"He's the only one who could do something like that. That's all. Come on, let me brush your hair. It's gotten all messed up"

Nixa snorted but walked over and sat down in front of her maid. "What's the point? I doubt those guards will allow me to leave."

Benodin picked up the brush and ran it through Nixa's hair. "You never know. You need to be ready for anything."

Nixa turned in her chair and grabbed Benodin's arms. "You've got to find out what's happening! If Vrag's alright."

Benodin's hand stilled. "Very well. If I do, will you let me fix your hair?"

Nixa nodded. Benodin pulled the bell chord by the bed. "Someone'll be here in a few moments. I'll talk to them. Now," she put her hands on the sides of Nixa's face and turned her toward the mirror. Neither girl spoke again as Benodin arranged her hair. Finally, a knock sounded on the door, and a servant entered with a food tray. As soon as the guards closed the door on the new servant, Benodin pounced.

"What news, Marnie?"

The girl sat the tray on the table and plopped onto one of the chairs. "Duke Burig's captured the king. He's had him taken to the dungeons."

Nixa gasped. "Is he hurt?"

"He had some minor wounds," the girl replied with a sad smile, "but as far as I know, he's alright." Marnie and Benodin exchanged glances. Nixa saw and shuddered.

"But he probably won't stay that way for long, will he?" she asked.

Marnie just shook her head.

"I don't understand," Nixa said. "How is it possible? How could he have taken over the castle without us hearing any fighting?"

Marnie shifted her feet and avoided Nixa's eyes.

"What is it?" the princess asked. "Tell me."

"The Queen of Penningdon helped him."

Nixa's lips pressed together in a tight line.

"Somehow, a great number of human soldiers snuck in," Marnie continued. "With their help, Duke Burig's men just went through the castle, taking the guards out one and two at a time. Any that were in visible locations, he replaced with his own until all the king's loyal men had been captured, and only the traitors remained. With Captain Uenk gone and King Vrag missing, there was no one to stop them."

"It was that easy?" Nixa asked incredulously.

Marnie nodded.

All of a sudden, Nixa's eyes grew hard. "Is the queen here?"

Marnie nodded again, then stood and ran her hands down her dress. "I need to get back before they send someone after me."

When she left, Nixa jumped to her feet and began pacing the room. "We need to do something."

Benodin turned and watched her helplessly. "What can we do?"

"We need to find some way to rescue Vrag and get rid of Stelia and her soldiers."

Benodin laughed humorlessly. "And how can we do that?"

Nixa stopped and stared at her. "If Vrag's in the dungeon, they probably don't see him as much of a threat anymore. Do you think?"

"Maybe not as much of one. If he's locked up. But they know he's dangerous. They won't lower their guard completely. If they torture him, though, he'll be weak. He won't be as able to fight back."

Nixa cringed at that thought.

"But what if he wasn't weak? If they lower their guard a little, and he isn't as helpless as they think, maybe he'll have the element of surprise. Maybe he'll be able to escape."

"But he is weak. Or he will be. There's no way the duke won't torture him now that he has him under his control. The man loves watching people suffer too much."

Nixa took a deep breath. "Do you remember when you told me about the blood bond?"

Benodin narrowed her eyes. "Yes." She drew the word out cautiously.

"You said it enabled two people to share their life forces. If he shared my life force, could he draw on my strength? Would it make him stronger?"

Benodin frowned fiercely. "Don't even think about such a thing! Don't you remember what could happen if it doesn't work? You could die. Immediately. Or you could be deformed and die slowly. It's too much of a risk."

"What will happen if Burig has control of the kingdom?"

Benodin took a deep breath. "He's an evil man. He would be a ruthless tyrant."

"And many people will suffer and die?"

"Yes, many people will suffer and die."

"Is there any other way to get rid of him?"

Benodin walked over to the window and gazed over the blue-lit cavern city as she thought.

Finally, Nixa could take no more of the silence. "There isn't any other way, is there?"

"I still say it's too risky. You don't even know if it'll work. Your human life force might not be strong enough to help. Perhaps... perhaps, I can take some drugged drinks down to the guards. Then, when they're knocked out, I can get their keys and set him free?"

"Would that work?" asked the princess doubtfully. Her guards in Penningdon would never fall for such a trick.

"No, probably not," the ogre girl reluctantly admitted. "Maybe I could get some of the other servants together, and we could find out where they're holding the other guards and free them."

"You don't think they killed them all?"

"No, Duke Burig would keep them alive. He wouldn't want to waste a resource, especially now that the human queen has been down here. He'd want to make sure he had enough soldiers to protect the city. After King Vrag is dead and he is crowned, he would assume the soldiers would switch their loyalties to him."

Nixa grimaced. "Do you think you would be able to free them?"

Benodin growled. "Probably not."

With a firm nod, Nixa replied, "Then this is the only option. We must give Vrag the strength to free himself."

"I don't like it. Besides, the potion might not even take hold."

"Why wouldn't it?"

"Both parties have to be willing to bond for it to work. You're willing, and I know the king cares for you, but does he care enough that he would be willing to bond with you?"

"You can't tell him! He'd never agree. If for no other reason, he might think it's too dangerous. Will it not work if you don't tell him?"

"It might if he loves you."

Nixa gasped. "Does he love me?"

"I don't know."

The two girls stared at each other, considering the implications.

"What if we try it, and he doesn't? Will it hurt me?"

"I don't think so. I think it just won't do anything. Your life is only in danger if the bonding takes hold and attempts to connect you."

"Then we'll try it. What do we need to do?"

Benodin sighed in defeat. "I'll need to get some of your blood and some of his. Then, I'll take it to a mage and have him make the potion for me."

"Do you know someone who'll make it without asking any questions?"

"I know someone."

"Good then, that's settled."

"Not really. First, I have to see if I can get his blood somehow. Here," she pulled the covers off the food Marnie brought. "If I'm going to be taking your blood, you need to eat something and build up your strength."

"Very well," Nixa sat and dipped her spoon into a delicious-smelling soup. "Do you have what you need here? Can you take my blood now?"

"No. I have to get his first. His is stronger. It'll need to be the base. Then, I'll pour yours over it."

As Nixa ate, Benodin unwrapped the bundle, revealing a shiny red apple. Nixa's eyes brightened when she saw it.

"I love apples! I haven't seen one since I've been down here. Where did you get it?"

Benodin took a knife and cut the fruit into small pieces. "My cousin brought it from the surface."

Nixa didn't notice how her voice shook, and her hand trembled as she placed the slices on the plate.

"Have you ever had an apple?" she asked.

Surprised by the question, Benodin replied honestly. "No, I haven't."

"Here, then," Nixa picked up a slice and held it out to the ogre. "Try it. You'll love it."

Benodin's heart skipped a beat. "No, no. I can't. My cousin sent these specifically for you. He'll kill me if I eat them." She forced out an unsteady chuckle.

"I won't tell him," said Nixa, still holding out the piece.

Benodin grabbed her wrist and pushed the fruit to Nixa's lips. "I insist. You eat them. I've heard that these can give special nutrients to people. They might help with the bond. They might help the king. You need to eat them. Go ahead. Eat them all."

She was babbling, but she couldn't seem to stop. She pushed the plate closer to the princess and turned away. Her eyes had begun to tear up, and she didn't want the human to see her weakness. Nixa shot her a puzzled look but did as she asked. She bit into one of the apple slices.

As soon as she swallowed the fruit, her eyes shot open wide. She took a few gasping breaths and then fell to the floor.

Tears streamed down Benodin's face as she knelt by her friend.

"I'm sorry. I'm so sorry. I'm so, so sorry." Sobs wracked her body. She lifted Nixa's limp form onto her lap and hugged her. "I'm sorry. I'm sorry. I'm sorry." Taking a shaking breath, she picked up the small human and carried her to the bed. She gently laid her down on the covers and spread her dress out around her.

"They have my sister," she choked out between sobs. "Duke Burig. He has my sister. He said he'd kill her if I didn't do it. I'm so sorry." She gently arranged Nixa's long ebony locks around her face. "You're not dead. He swore it wouldn't kill you. He said it'd just make you sleep. You're alright." She patted Nixa's shoulder. "I'm so sorry. Maybe... Maybe this is a good thing. Maybe your life force will be stronger when you sleep. You will be resting. You won't be using any energy. Maybe you'll have more to share this way. Maybe... Oh, I'm so sorry."

Benodin pushed herself off the bed and rushed out the door, past the bewildered guards.

# Chapter 13

V rag was thrown into a cold, damp cell in the murky depths of the dungeon. He lay there, his mind racing and his heart pounding. He should have known that Burig could not be trusted. Finally, he pulled himself to his feet, pain radiating throughout his body.

The darkness of his cell was oppressive. It did nothing to douse Vrag's anger and hatred for the traitorous duke. As he stood there listening to the silence, he thought about Nixa. Had Burig kept his promise? Had he released her? Or had he taken her as his own pet and done all the things he seemed to enjoy with pets he'd had in the past? Vrag slammed his fist into the wooden door. If that man so much as touched her, he'd kill him.

He heard footsteps approach and prepared himself to fight. A guard jerked the door open. Two others stood behind him with bows pulled taut and arrows pointed at the ogre king. With a growl, Vrag relaxed his stance. He allowed them to remove him from the cell and drag him down the hall. He knew what room stood at the end of the corridor.

The torture chamber.

It was rarely used under his rule. He didn't particularly enjoy causing pain, but it had been used from time to time when other means of acquiring information failed.

Vrag's hands were shackled to a wooden plank attached by chains to the ceiling. His legs were chained to hooks attached to the floor. The position allowed his torturers to come at him from the front or the back with ease. Eight guards surrounded him, swords drawn, and the archers stood ready, preventing him from trying to escape. The guards stepped away as Duke Burig entered the room. He seemed to revel in Vrag's misery and humiliation as he walked around him, examining his condition with an amused smirk on his face.

"Shall we begin?" he said in a cold voice.

At that moment, two of Burig's guards stepped forward and began flogging the ogre king with spiked whips. Every inch of his body felt like it was on fire as they lashed out against him with all their might. He could feel the whips cutting through flesh and muscle. The pain was almost unbearable, but Vrag refused to show any signs of weakness. He wouldn't give Burig the pleasure.

He gritted his teeth and held back the screams that threatened to escape him as the blows continued unrelentingly. His throat clenched with the effort, his breaths coming rough and uneven, forcing their way through his nose, flared with pain. After what seemed like an eternity, Burig finally called off the torture and nodded at the guards, who left the room without a word. Vrag sagged, the irons biting into his wrists as they bore his weight. Blood dripped onto the floor, soaking the torn remains of his shredded shirt.

With a grin, Burig leaned over Vrag's beaten body and whispered, "Your punishment is not over yet, but I'll give you a little break to regain your strength and look forward to what is to come."

Vrag glared up at him, his eyes filled with hatred and defiance. "Do your worst," he spat through gritted teeth.

Burig chuckled darkly. "Oh, I will. You truly are an impressive creature, Vrag. And for that, I think I'll reward you with a long life. I shall enjoy torturing you for years to come. You can be my new pet."

With that, he nodded to his men, who unshackled Vrag and dragged him away. The king tried to resist, but his body was too weak from the blood loss and pain. He was pulled from the room and thrown back into his cell. The guards secured him into the restraints and locked the door behind him.

Vrag tried to focus on anything other than the agony coursing through his body, but it was impossible. He had been injured in battle many times, but he had never felt pain like this before, and he knew that it was far from over. He lost track of time as he sat there, his mind drifting in and out of consciousness. At one point, he heard footsteps approaching. He didn't have the energy to lift his head to see who it was. The door to his cell opened, and he saw feet walking toward him.

"Your Majesty?" Benodin's voice came to him as through a haze. "What have they done to you?"

Vrag tried to look up, but the pain was too much. Benodin knelt beside the king and winced at the sight of his shredded back, chest, and sides. She pulled out some medical supplies and started tending to his wounds, cleaning away the dried blood and applying salves to help them heal. She carefully wrapped them with clean bandages. Vrag watched through swollen eyes as Benodin worked.

"Is Nixa safe?" he asked in a strained voice, dreading the answer.

Benodin's hands stilled for a moment, then resumed their work. Finally, she spoke, her voice soft and quiet. "She still lives."

Vrag tried to push himself to his feet, but his legs crumbled under him.

"She isn't hurt," Benodin insisted, pushing him back onto the cell floor. "You must rest and heal before you'll be any good to anyone. She will wait. I won't let Duke Burig hurt her. Here, drink this." She pressed a cup against his lips insistently. "It will help you heal."

Vrag reluctantly opened his mouth and accepted the bitter-tasting brew, and darkness began closing in on him. He heard her quiet steps retreat and the cell door close before the world went silent.

"You know that's useless," Duke Burig sneered at the maid as she hurried away from the king's cell. "He will continue being tortured until I grow tired of it."

"I would've thought that you'd want to kill him yourself rather than have him succumb to his injuries," Benodin replied. "Was I wrong?"

Burig snorted. "Fine. You can continue seeing to him, but if I discover that you're attempting anything you shouldn't, you will join him in the torture chamber." With a final snarl, he motioned for the guards to escort her out.

Benodin bunched the bloodied rags, all that remained of his shirt, into a light ball and held them carefully as she hurried back to Nixa's chamber. She cast one sorrowful glance at the bed where the beautiful human lay in her cursed sleep. The sleep she had condemned her to. She suppressed a sob. And now, she might be condemning her to an even worse fate.

Benodin slowly closed the door on the two humans standing guard in the hallway and locked it, pocketing the key. She heard a slight stirring from outside, but they didn't protest. Undoubtedly, they knew they could still enter if they needed to. It wouldn't take much for an ogre to break down the door.

She rushed over to the table and laid down the soiled cloth. She quickly emptied the goblet left over from lunch and winced as her eyes caught sight of the remainder of the apple lying on the plate beside it. She shook her head to banish the haunting and guilty thoughts.

Benodin picked through the rags and grabbed the bloodiest one. Holding the red-stained cloth over the goblet, she wrung it out, watching as Vrag's blood fell into the cup. Was it enough? She did the same with the rest of the bloodied rags to make sure.

When she had squeezed out as much of the crimson liquid as she could, she threw the cloth into the fireplace and turned to face the human. Her stomach churned as she stared at the helpless girl. Could she really do this? Should she do this? It was the last thing Nixa had asked of her, but...

If it went wrong, Nixa could die. Nixa would die. If she didn't do it, though, they could all die. Duke Burig was an evil, cruel man. If he were allowed to set himself up as king, he would be a tyrannical ruler. Nixa would never forgive her if she didn't try to help. She would never forgive herself.

Benodin picked up the dagger Nixa had left on the bed table and gently grabbed the girl's arm. She sliced a shallow cut and held it over the goblet. She felt sick as she watched her friend's blood spill into the cup. When she thought she had enough, she bandaged the wound, placed the goblet on the lunch tray, and opened the bedroom door.

The guards watched her leave as if she were no more than an insect crawling across the floor. Benodin headed back toward the kitchens but stopped when she came to a secluded hallway. She hurriedly set the tray on the floor behind a potted plant. She grabbed the goblet and rushed down a side passage and out a rarely used servant's door. With one hand holding a napkin to cover the goblet, she made her way to the home of a mage friend of hers. Even though she thought it was a foolhardy idea, she would fulfill Nixa's request. She would allow her friend this chance to try to save their king.

"You lied to me." Queen Stelia sat on the throne meant for the ogre queen and played with a lap full of jewels.

"How so?" asked Duke Burig, reclining beside her on the king's throne.

"You said the other ogres were stupid. They most certainly are not."

Burig shrugged. "Would you have worked with me if I had told you the truth?" He turned Vrag's crown over in his hands, watching the light reflect off the gemstones adorning it.

"Perhaps."

"Would you have helped me so soon?"

"No. I would have wanted to wait and do more recognizance first," the queen admitted.

"There, then. It seems I made the right decision. We won anyway, and we won quickly."

Stelia frowned at him. "I don't like being lied to, neither do I like being kept in the dark."

"But you do like shiny jewels." Burig lifted a handful of the gemstones from her lap and released them. They fell back among the others with a light tinkle.

Stelia grinned. "Yes, I like jewels."

Burig lifted the crown and set it on his head. "Then jewels you shall have."

"And Princess Nixa."

"And Princess Nixa," the duke agreed.

"Then, continued protection you shall have until you get your new reign fully established."

Burig reached over to shake her hand. "And thus, the alliance between Penningdon and Kelgrod is forged."

Benodin stood outside the heavy wooden door to the mage's secluded house, her heart pounding. She took a deep breath and raised her knuckles to knock. The door opened slightly before she could make contact, revealing a cloaked figure who peered at her with inscrutable eyes.

"Benodin," the mage's deep, resonant voice rumbled, "What brings you here?"

Benodin swallowed hard, her voice quivering as she replied, "I need your help, Master Thalnir. It's a matter of great urgency."

Thalnir opened the door wider, allowing her to step inside the dimly lit chamber. The room was adorned with mystical symbols, ancient scrolls, and arcane artifacts. The air was thick with the scent of various herbs and concoctions that lined the wooden shelves. The center of the room held a rough-hewn wooden table, upon which various glass vials, strange-looking plants, and a cauldron rested. The table was marred with scorch marks and worn from years of experiments.

Benodin stood by the table, her eyes fixed on the concoction bubbling in the cauldron. Her hair fell in disarray, and her face bore signs of fatigue and worry. The weight of her choices pressed upon her shoulders, and her hands trembled as she held the goblet containing the blood of Nixa and King Vrag.

"What troubles you, Benodin?" Thalnir asked, his eyes peering from beneath his hood.

Benodin hesitated. She was caught in a storm of emotions. The gravity of what she was attempting was overwhelming. Her loyalty to King Vrag battled with her determination to protect Nixa, creating a maelstrom of conflict within her. Regardless, she didn't dare reveal what was happening in the castle or who the recipients of the potion would be. She feared he wouldn't help her if he knew. She chose her words carefully.

"I came to get a marriage bond potion made," she said. Her pathetic attempt at a smile only managed to warn Thalnir that something was not right.

"What is it? What's wrong?" he asked.

"What do you mean?" Benondin wiped her sweaty hand on her gown, then switched the goblet to her other hand and wiped the other one.

"Who is the potion for?" asked Thalnir.

Benodin gulped. "I can't say," she replied sheepishly.

Thalnir narrowed his eyes. "Why not?"

The maid thought quickly. Various ideas came to her, but she dismissed them all as unconvincing. Thalnir's impatience showed on his face. She had to say something.

"They don't have their parent's permission," she blurted out.

Thalnir's brow furrowed. "So, they're not of age?"

"No, no. They're old enough. Their parents just don't approve. They're afraid they might try to stop it, so they want to marry in secret."

"You can't even tell me who they are?"

"Sorry," Benodin replied sheepishly.

"Alright, but if any trouble comes from this, you did not get the potion from me."

Benodin's smile was genuine this time. "I don't even know who you are."

Thalnir grunted and held out his hand for the goblet.

The mage mixed the ingredients, his movements precise and efficient. Benodin watched with bated breath as the potion took shape. With each added ingredient, it shimmered and changed color, shifting from deep crimson to a ghostly blue and then to a luminous violet. The room felt alive with energy, and the pressure of the magic was palpable. Benodin's heart raced with hope. The fragile thread of optimism intertwined with the fear that gnawed at her insides.

As the potion neared completion, Benodin's breaths came in shallow gasps. The mage's movements became slower and more deliberate, the final touches of his mystical craft coming together. And then, with a final incantation, the potion took on a brilliant, ethereal glow.

# Chapter 14

Benodin returned to the castle with the empty goblet and a vial of potion. The tension in her chest weighed her down, the gravity of her actions pressing heavily upon her conscience. Once in the castle, she stopped by the kitchen and made up a tray with a bowl of broth and a goblet of water. She didn't want the guards to be suspicious about her returning to Nixa's rooms so soon after she had left.

As she entered the dimly lit chamber where the princess lay trapped in the enchanted sleep, Benodin's heart ached. She felt like a murderer approaching her victim. And, potentially, she was. If this went wrong... If she caused her death...

She set the tray on the table and walked over to the bed. Gently stroking Nixa's hair, she whispered, "Are you sure about this, my friend?"

The girl made no movement, but Benodin felt a sense of expectancy fill the air as if the human's spirit hovered over her, urging her on. With a deep sigh, Benodin took the bowl of broth off the tray and tried to feed a spoonful to the girl. The potion was too precious to waste until she knew the princess could swallow in that condition.

She pressed the spoon between her lips and emptied it in her mouth. Nixa instinctively swallowed, and Benodin sat back, both relieved and horrified.

Relieved that she would be able to drink the potion.

Horrified that she would be able to drink the potion.

With a deep breath, Benodin drank the water, emptying the goblet. She opened the vial and poured the potion into the cup. She filled the spoon and again placed it between Nixa's lips.

She fed her half the potion and sat back and waited. Would she be able to tell if it was working? Would it even do anything before Vrag drank?

As she watched, a slight glow formed around the sleeping princess. It only lasted a few seconds before it faded away. This sent a new urgency rushing through the ogre maid. Was there a time limit to the potion?

She jumped to her feet, almost knocking over the goblet in her haste. With a gasp, she steadied the precious object and set it back on the tray. She took a moment to regain control of her features before opening the door and waltzing out past the guards.

As soon as she turned a corner out of sight, she grabbed the goblet more securely and hurried toward the dungeons, only slowing down when she reached the door. She casually strolled in and glared at the guards when they stopped her.

"I'm here to bring King Vrag something to eat," she announced, holding out the tray with the broth and the goblet placed prominently at the front.

The guards exchanged glances but seemed to have no reason to doubt her. With a dismissive wave, they allowed her to pass. Benodin made her way to Vrag's cell, where the king lay, barely conscious, his body battered and bruised.

He was worse. The bandages she had so carefully wrapped a little more than an hour ago were gone. In their place were more lacerations, more contusions, more blood.

She knelt beside him, careful not to touch him. There didn't seem to be any part of his body that hadn't been mangled or ripped to shreds. Benodin shuddered at the sight. Any doubts that she had about what she was doing suddenly fled. She loved her human friend and didn't want to see any harm come to her, but this was bigger than them. If Duke Burig could do this to his king, there would be nothing he wouldn't do to the common people of Kelgrod.

The only hope for their kingdom was for Vrag to regain control. And his only chance of that was to bond with the princess and share her life force. Her strength. Her power. She was only a human, so it wouldn't be as powerful as that of an ogre, but she had a strong spirit. Hopefully, it would be enough to boost his natural healing abilities.

"Your Majesty," Benodin whispered as she entered his cell, "I've brought you something to eat."

Vrag's eyes struggled to focus, but he recognized Benodin's voice. His voice was weak and hoarse as he croaked, "I can't..." He struggled feebly against the chains securing him to the prison wall.

"Here," she said, holding out a spoonful of the broth. With the shape he was in, he might not be able to drink any more easily than Nixa. She would see how he did with the broth first.

He didn't seem able to hold his head up, so Benodin pressed the spoon against his lips with one hand and helped raise his head with the other. He immediately coughed up the first spoonful, and panic raced through the maid. What if he couldn't drink it?

After his coughing fit subsided, she tried again. This time, the broth went down smoothly. Did she dare try the potion yet? One more spoonful of broth first, she decided. When that one went down as well, she picked up the goblet. But King Vrag turned his head away.

"Enough," he said weakly.

Benodin's breath froze in her throat. "Just take a few sips of this, Your Majesty. It will give you strength."

"Is this one of your infernal potions?" he growled out between gasps for air. The effort caused him to begin coughing again, and Benodin waited for him to regain his breath.

"Sort of," she replied when he was silent once more. "It will help you. I promise."

"What's the point?" he breathed out barely above a whisper.

"Now, now. I'll not have that kind of talk." She pressed the goblet against his lips and held his head back. Reluctantly, he let her pour the potion into his mouth. For a moment, she feared he would spit it out, but he didn't. He swallowed. Before he could protest again, she made him drink the rest of it. Then she sat back and waited.

It had only taken a few moments for the princess to glow. It shouldn't take long for her to see results with the king. But nothing seemed to be happening. Her eyes roamed his body, searching for a sign that it was working. Any sign. Had the bonding failed? Was Nixa dying in her chamber as she sat there?

Just as she was about to jump up and check on the human girl, she saw it. One of the deep gashes across Vrag's naked chest slowly began to close. Her eyes eagerly searched the rest of his body. Everywhere, wounds were closing, bruises were fading, and burns were healing.

The king sat up straighter and stretched his back. He cracked his neck from side to side and gave the maid a stern look.

"What exactly was in that potion?"

Benodin laughed. A bit hysterically. It worked. If Nixa had died or been deformed, King Vrag wouldn't be able to draw on her life force like this. It had worked. She wanted to jump up and run around the cell, laughing. She wasn't a murderer. They just might be able to save the kingdom after all. She tried, unsuccessfully, to stop the spread of the smile taking over her face. Now wasn't the time to rejoice. Vrag still stared at her, waiting for an answer. She just giggled.

"Does it matter? It worked. Now, go reclaim your kingdom and rescue your human."

That was all the reminder he needed. With a last suspicious glance, Vrag rose to his feet and, with one mighty yank, pulled the chains from the wall.

The action was not a silent one. Two guards immediately ran to his cell, swords drawn. Using the chains as whips, he quickly disarmed them. Benodin turned and looked away as he silenced the traitors forever.

"Your Majesty." The cry came from one of the other cells. Vrag recognized the voice as one of his personal guards. He bent down and took the ring of keys from the dead traitor's belt.

"How many of you are down here?" he asked as he unlocked the guard's cell.

"Four in here," the man replied.

"Five down here," came a call from another cell.

"Three in here," came another cry.

Voices of his faithful men rang up and down the dungeon. Vrag released them all. They took the dead guards' swords and daggers and collected their bows from the guard room. But some of Vrag's men had to leave the dungeons without weapons. Vrag, himself, carried nothing but his chains. He had unlocked them, but he took them with him. They would make adequate weapons until he could replace them with better ones.

They quickly ascended the stairs to the upper levels of the castle. He would bet anything that Duke Burig would be in the throne room—sitting on his throne. No doubt with that human queen beside him. Some of her soldiers had eagerly participated in his torture, and he was looking forward to repaying the favor.

They spread out. The element of surprise was their only chance with so few numbers. Vrag directed some of his men to the barracks. That would be the most likely place where Burig was holding the other soldiers. He wasn't a fool. He wouldn't have killed them all, and there was no better place to imprison such a large number of men. If they could free them without sounding an alarm, they stood a much better chance of success.

He sent a few more throughout the castle to take out any guards they found wandering around. The rest, he had follow him. If they could capture the duke and the queen, their soldiers would fall in line. He would have to be quick, though. He had no way of knowing if Burig still had the deadly collar around Nixa's neck. He would have to take him out before he had time to do anything.

Vrag's men moved through the castle silently, making quick work of any guards that stood in their way. Vrag led the charge, moving towards the throne room with his eyes scanning the corridor for any sign of the enemy. But as they approached the Great Hall, Vrag heard the sounds of a large gathering. Loud cheers and music filled the air. That could only mean one thing. They were celebrating. And with celebration came drink.

"Your Majesty, we should retreat and devise a plan," one of his men whispered.

But Vrag shook his head. It sounded like a significant number of soldiers were inside, but if they were drunk, they would be less able to fight.

"No. We must strike now while they're unprepared," he said. "We have the element of surprise. We can do this."

He instructed his men to sheath their swords. Those who had taken weapons from guards they had killed stuck them through their belts as well as they could. They would enter the room pretending to be part of the group and spread out among the humans. The human soldiers wouldn't recognize them as quickly as the ogres would, and they would keep their element of surprise longer.

Vrag would enter the room from the back, behind the head table on the dais. He would attempt to sneak up behind Burig and take him out quickly. The few men with him would capture the queen and take care of anyone else at the head table who might cause trouble. With those two under control, the other men should be able to easily subdue the rest of the room.

They put their plan into motion. Everything went smoothly until Duke Burig recognized one of the ogre warriors wandering between the tables. He jumped to his feet, but before he could cry out, Vrag came up behind him and slammed his chains against the back of the man's head. Burig collapsed to the ground with a thud.

Queen Stelia, sitting beside him, gasped, but she didn't have time for any other reaction. As soon as Burig's body slid to the ground, Vrag was behind her with a dagger pressed against her neck.

Chaos erupted in the room but quickly subsided when Vrag held up his free hand for silence.

"Listen well," the king shouted, his deep voice echoing through the hall. "My men have retaken the castle. Surrender now, and no one else will be hurt," he declared. "Much," he added as an afterthought.

The human soldiers looked around, unsure of what to do. Queen Stelia, still held captive by Vrag, looked up at him with fear in her eyes. "Please, spare my life," she begged. "I can be of use to you."

Vrag considered her offer. Killing her would only cause unnecessary trouble, and he did need someone to run the human kingdom for him since he planned on keeping Nixa. "If you swear loyalty to me and my people, I will spare your life," he said.

Stelia nodded vigorously, relieved to have been given a chance at survival. "I swear loyalty to you and your people," she said, her voice trembling.

"Take her to the dungeons," he ordered his men, gesturing towards the queen. "We have work to do."

As the men dragged the human woman away, the rest of Vrag's warriors who had been rescued from the barracks rushed into the hall. The king ordered them to secure the prisoners and left them to their task. He needed to check on Nixa.

Something was wrong. The feeling hadn't gone away after he escaped from the dungeon. And it hadn't gone away after he and his men captured Duke Burig and the queen. If anything, the feeling intensified as he rushed toward his chambers.

He slung the door open and ran into Nixa's room. She wasn't there. He stormed back out into the hall.

"Where is she?" His voice thundered down the corridor. A nearby servant bowed low, her frame shaking. "They took her to her old bedroom."

Before she had even finished speaking, Vrag pushed past her. He tore into Nixa's chambers like a wild animal but skidded to a stop when he saw her still figure lying on the bed. He stared in shock, then turned accusing eyes to Benodin.

"You said she hadn't been hurt."

"She hasn't," Benodin replied, tears streaming down her face.

Vrag slowly approached her, his face as pale as a ghost's. He fell to his knees beside the bed.

"She's dead." His voice trembled, and his hand shook as he reached for her.

"No. No," said Benodin, kneeling beside him. "She's not dead."

It took a moment for the words to register in the king's numb mind. When they did, his head jerked around to face her. "What do you mean? She isn't breathing. Her heart isn't beating. I would hear it. I would know."

"Yes, you would know," Benodin replied sternly. "Ignore the evidence of your eyes and ears. Listen to your heart. Is she dead?"

Vrag stared at the human girl who had so slowly crept into his affections. Suddenly, he leaned up and bent over her. "No," he said. "She isn't dead!"

His gaze shifted to Benodin. Awe brightened his eyes. "Despite the evidence, I know it. How do I know it?"

Benodin gulped and hesitantly told him about the bonding potion. As she expected, Vrag's face grew stormy with his rage. But his voice remained low when he spoke. Dangerously low.

"You should not have done that." His calm tone made Benodin's gut tighten. "You had no right to do that without my permission, and I would never have given it."

"It was her wish," the maid replied. "She wanted to help you. She... she cares for you." She started to say more, but his thunderous expression stilled her lips.

"And I care for her. That is what you want to say, isn't it? Otherwise, the potion wouldn't have worked."

Benodin nodded slowly.

Vrag growled and gazed down at Nixa. He brushed a strand of hair away from her face. Love filled his eyes, and the fury melted from his expression to be replaced with sorrow and pain.

"I would never have allowed it. Look what it has done to her. I have lost her."

Benodin's head fell into her hands, her shoulders shaking with her sobs. "Your bond didn't do this to her," she cried. "I did."

Surprised, Vrag watched her trembling body. There must be something more to her grief than forcing the bond on him, especially if that wasn't what caused Nix's current comatose state.

"Explain."

Benodin raised her red, puffy eyes and sniffed. "He kidnapped my sister," she said, pleading for him to understand. "Burig. He had his guards grab her from her home. He threatened to kill her if I didn't do it."

Vrag's brows lowered threateningly. "What did you do?"

Benodin turned her eyes back to the princess. "I tricked her into eating a cursed apple."

Vrag glowered. "What exactly did the curse do?"

Benodin waved her hand helplessly at the girl on the bed. "This is all I know. Well, this and that Burig said it wouldn't hurt her. He said she would only fall asleep."

"That doesn't sound like much of a curse." Vrag grabbed Nix by the arms and gently shook her. She didn't react. He shook her a little harder. She still didn't respond. He pinched her arm. Nothing. His lips pressed together tightly. "Did he say how she could be woken?" he asked through gritted teeth.

Benodin shook her head.

A scuffle in the hallway took their attention away from the problem. The bedroom door burst open, and a guard entered, followed by two more fighting to control a struggling dwarf. There were sounds of another in the hallway as well.

"We found these dwarves in the castle, Your Majesty. They say they have news about a curse someone's trying to inflict on the human princess." The guard's eyes found Nixa lying on the bed, and he gasped.

Brulin stilled as he saw her, too. "We're too late."

Even on his knees, Vrag towered over the shorter man. He scowled, hating to ask a dwarf for help, but he would do anything to save this girl who had so surprisingly become an integral part of his life. His very being. "Tell me everything you know," he said.

The dwarf glanced back at his brother in the hallway, still being restrained. "Release my brother. Let us see her, and I'll tell you."

Vrag ground his teeth in frustration but nodded. Thondrak shrugged the guards' hands away and walked over to the bed. Brulin followed him. He carefully took one of Nixa's hands in his and patted it awkwardly.

"What's wrong with her?" he asked.

"You mean, you don't know?" asked Vrag with a scowl.

"We heard she was to be cursed, not what the curse was."

"She's only asleep. The problem is, we can't wake her. Is there anything else you know? What can you tell me?"

Brulin told him what they had overheard in the guardhouse and about his other brothers going after Adrian to find out more. "The curse came from the human queen. She might know how to break it."

Vrag jumped to his feet. He shot the dwarves a cautious glance. It was evident by their actions and behavior that they cared for the girl. Still, he left two guards behind as he made his way to the dungeons. If the

172

queen knew how to break the curse, she would tell him. He had a torture chamber that would guarantee that.

# Chapter 15

Vrag leaned back against the stone wall and crossed his arms. "I've never been one to like torturing helpless females," he said. "But Mordag doesn't mind. That's why I invited him to join us."

Queen Stelia glanced at the huge ogre flexing his large muscles in his sleeveless shirt. Her eyes widened in horror.

"You see," said Vrag, walking across the room to where the frightened lady was chained to a table. "I don't like it when people hurt what is mine, and Nixa is mine." Vrag patted Mordag on the shoulder, and the man moved to a table covered with knives, whips, and other instruments of torture, some still stained with the ogre king's blood.

Stelia's eyes followed him as he picked up one instrument after another, examining them, choosing which would be the best to begin with.

"And you have hurt her," said Vrag.

Mordag decided on a scalpel. He ran his finger lightly over the blade and smiled when a bead of blood followed its progress.

"Ah, good. You're ready," said Vrag, smiling at the large man.

Queen Stelia gasped and tried to scoot away as he walked toward her, but her chained arms prevented her from moving far.

"What do you want?" she asked, panic filling her voice. "I'll give you anything. I'll—I'll even give you the Kingdom of Penningdon. Just don't hurt me."

Vrag held up his hand, and Mordag stopped, a frown on his face, the scalpel hovering over the queen's arm.

Vrag stood and glared at the small human, his feet spread apart, and his arms crossed. His bearing was the absolute image of power and strength. And determination.

"I already have Penningdon," he replied harshly. "What else will you give me?"

Stelia gulped. "Anything."

"Anything?"

Reluctantly, she nodded.

Vrag leaned down over her and sneered. "I want Nixa back, awake and unharmed."

"But—but," stammered the queen. "I—I don't know how to break the curse."

"Then, you can't give me what I want, can you?" He turned his back on her and walked toward the door. "Have fun, Mordag," he said as he left the room.

"Wait! Wait!" Her screams followed him down the corridor.

Vrag sat on the bed beside the sleeping princess, running his hand through her hair. The familiar gesture grounded him somewhat as he stared at the silken strands falling through his fingers. When had he begun caring so much for this human girl? When had she wormed her way so wholly into his heart? When had she changed from his pet to his heartbeat? His soul. His reason for living.

Ogres didn't cry—especially ogre kings—but Vrag's eyes stung. What if she never awoke? How would he go on living? How would he go on breathing? As it was, every inhale and exhale felt like a thousand-pound weight bearing down on his chest. He cupped her cheek with his large hand. She seemed so tiny. So helpless. So fragile.

Once again, Vrag tried to force some of his strength through their bond. He could feel her soul connected to his, but he couldn't reach her. If only he could give her some of his life force, maybe it would be enough to help her defeat the curse. But he couldn't. It was as if there were a brick wall keeping him out.

"I'm so sorry, my love," he said, stroking her face. "I failed you. I should have seen what Burig was planning. I should have been more careful. I grew careless. I should never have let you out of my sight."

He leaned down and rested his forehead against hers. "You mustn't give up hope. I have every scholar in the kingdom searching for a cure, and I've sent an entire battalion to Penningdon to bring back this Adrian. According to the dwarves, he knows how to break the curse. I *will* free you, and then you'll marry me and become queen of the ogres." Vrag let out a rough laugh. "That should turn this kingdom on its head. We'll have a fun time shocking all the members of my court. We'll dance inappropriately close at balls and make out before meetings. We'll have everyone gossiping about us for years. They'll never get over the scandals we'll create. An ogre king and human queen. We'll go down in history.

As what, I'm not sure." He laughed again. "But we'll go down in history as something."

He laid his head by her shoulder and slung his arm over her, pulling her close. "Rest well, my little human, while you can. You'll need your strength when you wake."

Nixa screamed in her mind. She, too, could feel the bond with Vrag, but she couldn't reach him either. The curse was blocking their connection somehow. Her body felt weak, so weak. And tired. She couldn't tell if it was from the curse or from when she had shared her life force with her ogre.

She felt his attempt to return strength to her, but for some reason, her body couldn't assimilate it. Perhaps her body couldn't take in the stronger power of an ogre. Perhaps the curse was protecting itself. Perhaps, a lot of things. Whatever the reason, she felt like she was disconnected. Floating. Nothing more than a powerless, helpless phantom trapped in the shell of her body.

She wanted so desperately to reach out and touch him. To comfort him. To tell him that everything would be alright. Her heart had soared when he called her his love. She chuckled when he painted the picture of their future together. He was right. His court would be scandalized when he married her.

Her soul warmed at the thought. She loved him. She loved him so much. Her big possessive, aggravating ogre. If only she could tell him how she felt. For the millionth time, she tried to move her body, open her mouth, anything. All she could do was lie there, relishing the feeling of his fingers running through her hair. If she could cry, she would have.

She felt the weight of his arm across her stomach and his hand holding tightly to her waist. It was a little too close to her backside, to be honest. She would have to have a talk with him about that when she woke. When they married, he could touch her there whenever he wanted, but until then, he should know better. Her body warmed at the thought of what he would do to her after they got married, but she quickly banished those thoughts from her mind.

How had she come to this point? Only a few months ago, she had been a pampered princess, chasing after any and every handsome lord she saw. She had been willing to murder to get what she wanted, even if all she wanted was the undivided attention of a particular man. She hadn't cared for anyone other than herself, not even the men she chased. She just wanted them to admire her.

It had taken her whole world crumbling down for her to see herself clearly. For her priorities to change. Would she be so ready to murder now? Nixa pondered the thought. If someone tried to hurt this man, definitely. If someone tried to hurt her dwarves, definitely. Had she really changed then? Had she grown at all?

She thought about it. She wouldn't kill anyone just to get them out of the way as a romantic rival. She wouldn't kill anyone just to gain power. She would only kill to protect those she loved. Yes, she thought. She had changed, but she still had a long way to go. Well, she thought with a snort. She had plenty of time now to think about it.

She felt Vrag's hand moving. He was rubbing her side in a gentle, comforting motion. It felt nice. Relaxing.

But the man was definitely getting too close to her booty. Yes, she was going to have to have a talk with him later.

Garroth squeezed into the narrow space between the houses and ran his hand over the stone wall. It felt solid and smooth. With a frustrated grunt, he snuck out of the alley and edged along the street toward the next. His stomach growled in protest at the lack of food he'd been giving it. They were still stuck inside the city and had been for days, eating and drinking whatever they could find. They didn't dare show their faces even though most of the soldiers had either gone after Nixa earlier or were chasing the other dwarves.

He and his brothers had decided the best way to escape would be to find a weakness in the city wall. If they could find even the slightest flaw in its design or chip in its mortar, they should be able to dislodge a stone or two and crawl through.

Unfortunately, Queen Stelia seemed to keep a well-maintained barrier against the outside world. They had spread out all through the city, meeting up each dawn to share news of their progress or lack thereof. Garroth sighed as another section of the stone boundary proved to be solid.

Just before he stepped out into the street to try another area, he heard a great commotion coming down the road. Moving back into the shadows, he waited for it to pass. His eyes widened in shock as he took in the strange sight coming toward him. It was ogres—ogres and one human prisoner. They were heading toward the castle.

That could only mean that the queen had failed in her attack. Could Nixa be safe? Had his brothers arrived in time? He hesitated for only a moment before he stepped into the street. He held up his hands in peace.

"My friends," he cried. "Do you come from Kelgrod?"

The ogre procession stopped.

"Yes," the leader replied. "Do you know a dwarf named Brulin?"

"He is my brother."

"Then you are the one seeking the way to break the curse. Has your mission been successful?"

"Yes. Unfortunately, we haven't been able to leave the city to deliver our news. Could you help us with that?"

"We most certainly can. You will be welcomed with great enthusiasm in the ogre kingdom." The man jumped off his large horse and approached the dwarf, leading his horse behind him. His immense size towered over the shorter man. "Come," he said. "It will be faster if you ride.

Garroth gazed up at the gigantic horse and cocked an eyebrow at the ogre. The large man laughed. "Would you be offended if I assisted you onto my steed?"

Garroth gritted his teeth but saw no other option. There was no way he could mount that giant animal on his own. If it weren't for his need to reach Nixa, he would never go near such a freak of nature. He reluctantly nodded, and the ogre quickly picked him up and threw him on the animal's back.

Garroth grabbed onto the saddle horn for dear life. It was a long way down if he fell.

"We need to find my brothers first," he said as the man turned to head back to the gate.

"Where are they?"

"Not far. I'll show you."

"How many?"

"Four."

Two other ogres dismounted and handed their reins to the first one. Then, they and the rest of the group broke away with their prisoner and continued to the castle.

"Lead the way," said the ogre.

Garroth took them around the city until they found the dwarves. Each of them looked horrified at the idea of having to ride the monstrous mounts. All except Harnic. He didn't even try to stop the smile that spread across his face.

They encountered no resistance as they approached the city gate this time. The ogres had informed the guards of the fate of their queen, and the frightened humans did nothing to stand in their way. As terrifying as the large horses were, at least they would make good time. They could finally get back to the princess and share their news. The question was would it do any good.

Queen Stelia huddled in the back of her cell, rubbing her bandaged arms. That horrible ogre had been playing with her, taunting her. The shallow cuts he had made along her arms stung, but she knew it wasn't nearly as bad as it could have been. Not nearly as bad as the rumors she had heard of how ogres tortured their captives.

He was only toying with her. That much was clear. But why? What did he hope to gain? Maybe he knew there wasn't any information he could get from her. Perhaps he wasn't even trying to get information. Maybe he was just a sick, sadistic basmod that liked to mess with people.

She had no doubt the torture would grow worse. The ogre king seemed to really like Nixa, and she had cursed her. She had also worked with his enemy to take over his kingdom. Burig had told her how he'd treated the man in the torture chamber. No, King Vrag wouldn't let her get away with what she'd done.

She almost wished the insufferable lout had just gotten it over with. The expectation of what was to come was driving her crazy. She rubbed her arms again. The cuts inched painfully. No, she didn't want it to get worse. Mordag could draw it out as long as he wanted to. She could handle the humiliation, but she didn't know if she could handle the pain.

In the midst of Vrag's silent vigil, the door to the chamber burst open with an echoing crash. A hoard of dwarves rushed into the room with an air of urgency, and the ogre king jumped up from his seat. He stared at the men, his massive form imposing and regal, as he impatiently awaited their news. But they just stood there, staring at the princess.

"What is it? Have you found a way to break the curse?" he implored.

Garroth stepped forward and nodded solemnly, his eyes still resting on his sleeping friend.

His sister.

"Yes. It can only be undone by true love's kiss."

The room fell into a stunned silence as Vrag processed the revelation. True love's kiss. The words echoed in his mind, and he gazed down at the girl he loved more than anything in the world. His heart pounded in his chest, and the realization bloomed within him. He knew he loved her. He had loved her for a long time. He could wake her. That is if she loved him back.

Vrag leaned down, his massive form hovering over the small girl, their faces inches apart, his heart and mind in turmoil. He longed to be the one who would break the curse, the one who would wake her from this eternal sleep. But did she love him? Could she love him? The one who had held her prisoner and treated her so badly. Was it possible?

Carefully, with trembling hands, he closed his eyes and pressed his lips tenderly to hers, a kiss filled with all the love and longing that flowed through his being. He could feel the tension in the room, the eyes of the dwarves upon them, and his heart raced as he poured all his affection into that tender gesture.

For a heartbeat, nothing happened. The room waited as if the building itself froze in suspense and hope. Vrag's own breaths came out in short, anxious bursts. But then, as if the very room exhaled, a soft, trembling sigh escaped from Nixa's lips. Her eyes fluttered open, and the world seemed to come alive once again in a burst of color and sound.

Nixa blinked in confusion, her gaze focusing on the face of the ogre king. Unspoken emotions, their love and devotion, flowed through their shared bond. Her lips curved into a smile, and her eyes filled with the light of recognition and love. She whispered, her voice like a gentle melody, "Good morning, King Vrag."

A relieved grin spread across Vrag's rugged face, and he gathered Nixa into his arms, holding her close. "Good morning, my love."

# Epilogue

Nixa sat on the ogre queen's throne, which had been temporarily moved into the courtyard. She glanced up at the imposing ogre seated on the king's throne beside her and smiled at her new husband. Once she had awoken, only a week ago, Vrag had insisted on a short engagement. He hadn't wanted to wait until she was his, and she was glad for his impatience. She hadn't wanted to wait either.

He reached over and gently squeezed her tiny hand in his large one, intertwining their fingers. His gaze grew intense at the contact, and her cheeks warmed at the memory of the previous night, their wedding night. A blaze of love and desire flashed through their bond and set her body on fire. She suddenly grew hot, and every nerve in her body came alive. His smug grin widened as he noted her response. He moved their clasped hands closer to her and rested them on her thigh. Releasing her grip, he began rubbing her leg. Nixa froze, sensations shooting up from her leg to flood her body.

Nixa was brought back to reality by the loud bang of the herald slamming his staff on the platform to gain the attention of the crowd. She swallowed self-consciously, and her eyes shot out to meet those of the crowd, many of which were staring back at her, or rather, at the king's hand on her leg.

Her face turned even redder. She felt like she would be consumed by the heat burning through her. The heat of embarrassment. The heat of desire. What was wrong with her? She lowered her eyes, not able to bear their gazes.

"No, no, my love. You are the queen of the ogres. Don't be afraid to look them in the eyes." Vrag's gentle rebuke reminded her of her position. All the years of her princess training came back in a rush, and she lifted her head proudly. She squared her shoulders and gazed around the courtyard, meeting as many eyes as possible.

To her surprise, it wasn't anger that graced the majority of the faces. It was on some, naturally, but most of the ogres appeared more amused than anything else. Her face still flaming, she offered them all a smile.

"That's better." Vrag raised his hand, and the herald slammed his staff down once again.

"Bring out the prisoner," he cried out over the crowd.

Four guards exited the castle, surrounding the disheveled and filthy form of Duke Burig. Nixa gave the ogre king a sad smile. She was proud of him. Though the duke had spent the last week in the dungeons, he hadn't been tortured. Vrag hadn't sought revenge, only justice. She wasn't sure if she would have acted the same if she had gone through the torture her ogre had.

"Duke Burig Velspond, for the crime of treason against the Kingdom of Kelgrod, you have been sentenced to death," announced the herald. "Do you have any last words?"

Duke Burig's steely eyes rested on Vrag. He snarled and spit at the ground. The guards shoved him up onto the platform and pushed him down before the executioner, forcing his head on the chopping block.

Nixa glanced over to the left, where Queen Stelia and her soldiers stood surrounded by more guards, watching the proceedings. Hopefully, this would send a message to her that she wouldn't soon forget.

Nixa turned back to the duke just in time to see the axe fall. It was a gruesome way to spend the morning after their wedding, but it was necessary. The people needed to see what happened to traitors, and Penningdon needed to understand that they wouldn't easily find other allies in the ogre city.

As guards began pulling the duke's body away, Vrag stood and reached out a hand to Nixa. She took it and rose to her feet. Again, he raised a hand, and the guards surrounding Queen Stelia's party stood to attention. Stelia watched him warily.

"Take this as a warning." Vrag's voice thundered across the space to Penningdon's queen. "If you do not abide by our agreement, a worse fate shall befall you. And if any harm comes to our ogre ambassadors, we shall consider that a sign of rebellion and react accordingly. Do you understand?"

Nixa had never seen her stepmother so unroyal-looking. Vrag hadn't even given her the chance to clean up and change after her stay in the dungeon. Her hair hung limp and greasy, and her clothes were ripped and filthy from the dirty cell. He was definitely sending her and the people of Penningdon a message. Don't mess with the ogres.

Stelia nodded sheepishly. Pride and stubbornness alternated with fear and humiliation on her face. Nixa felt a flash of shame at the joy that raced through her at the sight. Apparently, she still had some maturing to do. But she was satisfied with their arrangement. Stelia was a good queen. Even if her actions had the wrong motives, the people were content under her rule. Nixa had her own kingdom to worry about now. She still felt a sense of loyalty to Penningdon and would step in immediately if the people were ever in danger, but she no longer had any desire to rule them, not directly, at least.

Under their new treaty, the queen was required to submit monthly state-of-the-kingdom reports to Vrag along with regular tribute. If the ogre king disapproved of any of the queen's actions, she would be required to change them.

He wasn't a complete tyrant, though. He would allow her to appeal his decision. All she had to do would be to personally compile a detailed report of her actions and the reasoning behind them, get statements from ten witnesses in the court and all the council members agreeing with her point of view, and have all of them journey to Kelgrod to present their case before the king. Hopefully, the hassle that would cause would be enough to prevent her from making hasty decisions that didn't benefit the people. For their part of the treaty, Kelgrod would fight for Penningdon in the case of unprovoked attacks from other kingdoms. Nixa thought it sounded fair.

She watched as the disgraced party, flanked by ogre soldiers and the ten ogre ambassadors on horseback, walked out of the courtyard and headed back to Pennindgon.

Nixa's eyes shot open wide as she felt a sharp pinch on her backside. Her gaze jumped up to the face of her husband, and her breath caught at the intensity of his stare.

"I'm confident you can take care of things for a few hours, Chancellor," he said, never taking his eyes off his new wife.

The chancellor, standing behind them, cleared his throat. "Of course, Your Majesty," he replied, amusement coating his words.

Vrag grabbed Nixa's hand, a world of promise in his eyes, as he pulled her back into the castle.

*The End*

Thank you for taking the time to read one of my books! I'm enjoying writing this series. I've had a love for fairytales ever since I was a child, and "Snow White" was always one of my favorites. Then *The Lord of the Rings* entered my life, and my love of fantasy grew. It's been amazing combining the elements of fairy tale and epic fantasy.

It would just thrill me to pieces if you would leave a review of this book on Goodreads or your favorite bookstore. I enjoy reading them. It makes me feel just a little bit more connected to all of you out there who share my love of reading and love of fantasy. Thanks in advance.

# Kingdoms of Beauty Series

www.ingramcontent.com/pod-product-compliance
Lightning Source LLC
Chambersburg PA
CBHW030222180626
46810CB00008B/2926